Rina's Family Secret

OTHER BOOKS IN
The Roosevelt High School Series

Juanita Fights the School Board

Maya's Divided World

Tommy Stands Alone

Rina's Family Secret

The Roosevelt High School Series

Gloria Velásquez

PIÑATA BOOKS
ARTE PÚBLICO PRESS
HOUSTON, TEXAS
1998

This volume is made possible through grants from the National Endowment for the Arts (a federal agency), Andrew W. Mellon Foundation, and the City of Houston through The Cultural Arts Council of Houston, Harris County.

Piñata Books are full of surprises!

Piñata Books
An Imprint of Arte Público Press
University of Houston
Houston, Texas 77204-2174

Cover illustration and design by Vega Design Group

Velásquez, Gloria.
    Rina's family secret / by Gloria Velásquez.
    p.   cm. -- (The Roosevelt High School series)
    Summary: A Puerto Rican teenager describes her family's life with her abusive stepfather in alternating chapters with the story of the counselor who is trying to help them.
    ISBN 1-55885-236-0 (clothbound : alk. paper).
    ISBN 1-55885-233-6 (trade paper : alk. paper).
    [1. Family violence — Fiction. 2. Family problems — Fiction. 3. Puerto Ricans — California — Fiction. 4. High schools — Fiction. 5. Schools — Fiction.] I. Title. II. Series: Velásquez, Gloria. Roosevelt High School series.
PZ7.V488Ri   1998
[Fic]—dc21   98-3218
                                                    CIP
                                                    AC

0 1 2 3 4 5 6 7   10 9 8 7 6 5 4 3 2

For Aunt Hope
and
all the brave women
at
The Women's Place
in Greeley, Colorado

One

Rina

I push my way through a group of students in the crowded hallway and hurry to my locker, hoping to leave the building as quickly as possible. As I sort through a messy pile of books and papers, someone taps me on the shoulder. I turn around to find Maya, Juanita and Ankiza standing behind me. "Hey," I mumble nervously, feeling as if I've been busted doing something I'm not supposed to be doing.

"Rina, we're all taking the bus over to the mall so that we can check out the new department store. You want to come with us?" Maya asks.

Maya is one of my best friends here at Roosevelt High. I've known her since she first came to live in Laguna. Maya's always the leader of the group, coming up with all kinds of crazy ideas.

"Well?" Maya asks impatiently.

I manage to tell the lie I'd been rehearsing. "Sorry. I need to go straight home, 'cause Mom's working late today and I told her I'd watch Joey and Carmen."

"What a bummer," Ankiza says.

Juanita is quick to add, "Just be glad you don't have to watch them every weekend, like me."

Ankiza gives Juanita a sympathetic look. Juanita has a bunch of younger brothers and sisters who she babysits while her parents work in the fields. Juanita's parents are poor like mine.

"At least you have brothers and sisters," Maya snaps. Maya's always feeling sorry for herself 'cause she's an only child. She turns back to me and says, "Okay, Rina, I'll call you later."

I wait until they've disappeared down the hallway. Then I grab my backpack and head for the nearest exit.

Outside, the campus is filled with noise and traffic as students take off in different directions. There are students dressed in baseball uniforms headed for practice. In the parking lot, there are groups of students hanging out, listening to music and smoking cigarettes. If there's one thing I can't stand, it's cigarettes. I remember when I was about twelve years old, one of my friends dared me to smoke a cigarette with her. I almost choked to death. Ever since then, I've hated smoking.

I've always liked coming to Roosevelt High. The only thing I hate is that there aren't too many blacks or Puerto Ricans. There are more Mexicans, or Chicanos, as Maya calls them. It used to bother me a lot when I was a freshman that I was one of the few Puerto Ricans at the school. But now that I'm a junior, I'm pretty much used to it. Most of the time, the teachers call me an "African-American" because my skin is so dark. I usually correct them, saying I'm Puerto Rican. It's not that I have anything against being called that. (Maya's boyfriend, Tyrone, always reminds me that I have African ancestry.) It's just that I'm very proud of being a *puertorriqueña*. Both my mom and my real dad are from Puerto Rico. They moved to New York from San Juan when I was a baby. Then, when I was about four years old, my real dad left us. Mom says he left her 'cause he was with another woman. So we ended up moving to Laguna to be near Abuela (that's my grandmother) and my aunt, *Titi* Carmen, who was working at an electronics plant in this area. Maybe if we'd never moved to Laguna, Mom wouldn't have met my step-dad, and things would've been different.

As I turn on Cabrillo street, I think about what happened this morning. Mom thinks I don't know what's going on, but I heard everything. I heard when she came in, mad as hell, and accused Dad of puncturing her tires so she wouldn't be able to go to work. Dad denied it all, like he always does. I heard him tell her, "I thought you said everyone liked you, that you don't have any enemies?" This made Mom even madder. When Dad started to laugh at her, Mom hollered back, "You're not going to stop me from going to work, José! If I have to walk, I'll get there." Then I heard her calling her friend, Marie, who works with her at the motel. Sometimes I really hate my dad. I don't know why Mom ever married him. I'm just glad that Carmen and little Joey were asleep and did-n't hear them arguing this morning.

I pause when I get to the ugly brown apartment com-plex where we've lived for the past five years. I sure hope Mom came straight home from work. Dad gets so mad when she's even a minute late, and then the hollering starts again.

We used to live across town close to Abuela but we moved here 'cause the rent's cheaper. Since Dad hardly ever works, we were able to qualify for government hous-ing. It's not so bad here. My friend Tommy lives in the next building, and Juanita and Tyrone live on the other side of the complex. Ankiza and Maya's parents have money, so they live where the rich people do, across town in big houses.

When I open the front door, my little brother comes running up to me. "Hey, Shorty," I say teasingly, giving him a big hug. Little Joey's real name is José Jr., like Dad, but we all like to call him Joey. It bugs the hell out of Dad, but I couldn't care less. Little Joey is eight years old and looks Mexican, like his Dad. He has Dad's wavy black hair and light-brown skin.

I say hello to my sister Carmen, who is sitting on the couch watching cartoons. Carmen is only ten years old, but she looks older 'cause she's so tall. Carmen and I both look like Mom. We have dark chocolate skin and the thickest, curliest black hair that drives us crazy in the morning.

I'm relieved when I find Mom in the kitchen making dinner. "Is Creepo home yet?" I ask rudely as I grab a

Coke from the refrigerator. Mom hates it when I call Dad names.

"*Cállate*, or you'll wake him," Mom scolds me. "He's taking a nap." I catch a glimpse of the deep worry lines that appear across Mom's forehead. Lately, they always seem to be there.

"I'll be upstairs in my room," I tell her, reaching for a couple of Oreos from the package sitting on the counter. I manage to avoid looking directly at Mom. The last thing I want is for her to look in my own eyes and see how bad I feel.

Upstairs in my room, I lie down and listen to my favorite radio station. When I'm finally relaxed, I force myself to do my algebra homework. It bugs me that it takes me forever to get through the problems. I just can't understand how Tommy and Maya can enjoy math so much. I hate it. If it weren't for their help, I'd probably never pass the tests.

I'm on my last equation when Carmen bursts into my room, telling me it's time to eat dinner. When I snap at her for not knocking, she sticks her tongue out at me, and then disappears before I have time to scold her. I hurry and put my shoes on, knowing that Dad gets angry if we're even a minute late for dinner. I wonder what kind of a mood he'll be in? I hope it's a good one, otherwise Mom will pay for it later.

When I walk into the dining room, everyone is already seated at the table, except for Mom who is heating up *tortillas*. One of the first things Mom had to learn to do for Dad when they got married was to cook *tortillas* and make *chile* . Everyday she makes fresh *tortillas* for him, even if she's sick.

"*¿Acabaste tu tarea?*" Dad asks me as soon as I sit down next to Carmen. I feel the tightening in my stomach start to relax. Whenever Dad asks me if I did my homework, I know he's in a good mood.

"It's cool, Dad," I answer, serving myself some of Mom's fried chicken and white rice. Out of the corner of my eye, I watch Dad. He's a handsome man with thick black eyebrows and a bushy moustache that makes him look very Mexican. Mom calls it his Emiliano Zapata moustache. Zapata was a hero of the Mexican Revolution a long time ago.

"*Qué bueno*," Dad says. Then he tells Carmen and little Joey, "See how smart your sister is? It's 'cause she does all her homework. You better follow her example."

"I will, *Papi!*" little Joey shouts.

Carmen smiles sweetly at Dad while she kicks me under the table. I kick her back, giving her a dirty look.

Mom finally sits down to eat with us. There is a tense, guarded look on her face.

"Alma, you're the best cook in town," Dad says, giving her a pat on the shoulder.

"*Ay*, José, you always say that," Mom answers in a tired, faraway voice.

"José, eat all your *verduras*," Dad orders little Joey, who scrunches up his face.

Carmen sticks her tongue out at him, but Dad quickly orders her to leave him alone. All the while, Mom is silent. It's almost as if she were invisible.

While we eat, Dad talks about the basketball playoffs and how he thinks the Lakers are going to make it to the finals. Little Joey gets excited and tries to talk with his mouthful, but he ends up spitting out a piece of carrot. We all laugh when Dad calls him a *cochino*.

After dinner, Dad tells Mom that he has some business to take care of and that he'll be back later. Mom nods her head obediently. But Dad doesn't fool me. I know that he'll be out all night with his drinking buddies. As soon as he leaves, Mom becomes a different person. While we watch TV, she smiles more and even talks about her work day. It bugs me that she's that way. Why can't she be this smart and lively when Dad's around? Why does she act so mousey and stupid when he's here?

When the phone rings, I race to answer it before Carmen has a chance to grab it.

"Hey, Rina. It's me, Maya. Want me to come over so we can do our Spanish homework together?" Maya's Spanish isn't so good and she's always asking for help with the homework from me or Juanita.

"I can't. I've got some stuff to do around the house."

"You sound weird, Rina. Is everything okay?"

There's one thing about Maya. She's very perceptive, almost as if she's psychic or something. "Everything's cool," I say.

"All right. Be anti-social. I'll see you tomorrow," Maya says, hanging up.

On an impulse, I dial Minerva's number. Minerva's only a freshman at Roosevelt, but lately I've started to hang out with her and some of her friends. Minerva's parents are Mexican and she lives over by City Park.

We talk for a few minutes before we agree to meet at City Park.

I'm headed for the front door when Mom stops me and asks, *"¿A dónde vas, hija?"*

"What do you care where I'm going?" I answer sarcastically. "You can't even keep track of your stupid husband." Then I walk away, slamming the door behind me as hard as I can.

Two

Rina

City Park is about four blocks from my apartment building. It's not the best-looking park. All the winos and homeless people gather there. I never used to hang out there, but one night I got tired of listening to Mom and Dad argue. So I took off walking and before I knew it I was at the park. Minerva was there with a group of friends that night and she right away called me over to join them. Ever since then, I've been meeting her at City Park whenever I get the chance.

When I get to City Park, I find Minerva standing around an old green Mustang, listening to the radio with some friends. As I get closer, I recognize Charley Maestas from my Spanish class. Everyone at school calls him a *cholo* 'cause he wears dickeys and talks weird Spanish or *pachuco* talk, as Maya calls it. I really don't care how he dresses or talks as long as he doesn't bug me.

"*Orale*, Rina," Charley says, giving me the Chicano handshake, which I manage to screw up.

"Hey, *baboso*," I tell him, and then I turn to greet Minerva, who is next to Sheena, smoking a cigarette. I remember how surprised I was the first time I saw Sheena at the park with Minerva. Sheena was the only *gringa* with a bunch of Chicanos. This bothered me because I thought about the fight she and Juanita had at school several years ago and how Sheena used to go around saying bad things about Mexicans and blacks. But that was a long time ago. Now Sheena's changed and acts pretty cool. Minerva says Sheena's poor like us and that she doesn't have a dad. Lucky her, I think to myself.

"Wanna smoke?" Minerva asks, waving a pack of Marlboros at me.

I tell her no, wondering why she always asks me if I want a cigarette. She knows I can't stand the thought of smoking. It reminds me of Dad. He always smells like cigarettes.

Although Minerva is fourteen years old, she looks about twelve. Minerva's small and weighs about a hundred pounds. She's not tall and big-boned like me. Minerva is always doing weird things with her hair. Last year she had it shaved on one side with one long bang hanging across her forehead. Now she's got it dyed orange red in a short punk-rock style.

"Hey, *esa*," Charley tells me, " saw your dad getting into a car with this hot-looking *ruca* the other day. What kind of work did you say he does?" A smirk spreads across his brown squarish face.

"My dad work? You've gotta be kidding," I answer sarcastically. "He's always out having a good time while my mom works."

"Turn it up, Charley," Sheena interrupts. "It's the new song by Prison Rage."

"Yeah, that song's hot," Charley says, moving closer to the car window so he can reach inside and turn up the volume on the radio.

I'm glad for the sudden interruption. The last thing I want to do is waste my time talking about Dad.

We're having a good time listening to music and watching the cars cruise around the park when I spot Tyrone's gray Maxima. As it rounds the block, it comes to a halt next to us. Tommy leans out the window, staring at me.

"Hey, Rina, what are you doing here?" he asks, a surprised look on his handsome face. I can tell by the sharp tone of his voice that it bugs the hell out of him that I'm in the park with Minerva.

"Same as you, just having a good time," I answer, walking up to the car.

"Get your butt home, Rina," Tyrone orders me from the driver's seat.

"Shut up, Tyrone," I holler back at him. Tyrone loves to boss everyone around. Every one except Maya, that is, 'cause she won't put up with none of that.

Just then another car pulls up. It's Mousey, another *cholo* friend of Charley's. "Hey, I gotta go," I tell Tommy. Before they drive away, he makes me promise to call him later.

When I go back, Minerva and Sheena are sitting on the patchy grass with Charley and Mousey. I can't help but stare at Mousey. I wonder if he got his nickname because of his pointy nose and small beady eyes that seem to dart in all directions.

Charley and Mousey are talking about last night's basketball game and how Michael Jordan scored forty points. Mousey is holding a bottle of Budweiser wrapped in a brown paper bag. He takes a long drink and then he passes the quart to Charley, who takes a long drink and then passes the bottle to Minerva. From there it goes to Sheena, and then to me. I never used to drink, but lately it's something I got started on.

By the time Mousey brings out another quart of beer, it's already dark outside except for the dim light coming from the street lamp, which is several yards away. We're starting to get a little buzz when a police car pulls up. Mousey is quick to hide the beer under his jacket. When the officer asks what we're doing, Mousey explains that we're just hanging out, listening to music. The officer flashes his light around us suspiciously. Satisfied that we're not doing anything illegal, he reminds us of the ten o'clock curfew, warning that he better not find us there after that hour or he'll take us in.

Once the police car is out of sight, Mousey pulls out the beer and passes it around again. By the time we finish it, I'm feeling real light-headed. When Mousey says he's going for more beer, I decide that I've had enough. I ask Minerva and Sheena if they want to walk home with me, but they tell me they're going to stay with the guys. Charley offers to drive me home, but I tell him no.

When I walk through the front door of the apartment, I'm startled to find Dad lying on the couch watching television. He's never home this early during the week. *"¿Dónde andabas, Rina?"* he asks, sitting up as soon as he sees me.

"I—I was at Minerva's house," I stammer.

"¡Mentirosa!" Dad yells, coming over to stand in front of me. "You were out whoring around like your mother, weren't you?"

I can tell that Dad's been drinking, because his speech is slurred and he's walking funny. "Look who's talking," I shout back angrily.

When Dad tries to grab me by the arm, I step back away from him and take off upstairs. I can hear him in the background, but I don't dare to look back.

As I open the door to my room, I catch a glimpse of Mom watching me through the crack in her open door.

Three

Rina

The next morning, by the time I've showered and dressed, Carmen and little Joey are downstairs watching cartoons. Mom always wakes them before she leaves for work. Carmen is supposed to help little Joey get dressed for school. I'm the one who makes sure they both eat their cereal and get to the bus stop on time each morning. When I get up late like today, Carmen helps little Joey get his cereal. Sometimes Dad is up early and he'll drive little Joey and Carmen to school. But this morning, he's still in bed. I'm glad because I have a slight headache and I don't feel like arguing with anyone.

At exactly seven-thirty, I tell Carmen to turn off the TV. Then I hand each of them their lunches and walk them to the front door. Little Joey always gives me a giant hug and kiss before he leaves. Then I stand and watch at the door until they've crossed the street to join the rest of the *barrio* kids who are waiting at the end of the block for the school bus.

Five minutes later, I grab my backpack and head for the stoplight at the front of the apartment complex, where I usually meet Juanita, Tommy and Tyrone. Ever since our freshman year, the four of us have walked together to Roosevelt High each morning. Once in a while, one of the guys gets his dad's car and gives us a ride. But I don't mind walking to school, except when it's raining. Maya and Ankiza, who live in the Laguna Hills area, are always telling us how lucky we are that we don't have to take the bus and sit with all the nerdy freshman.

Juanita is the only one waiting for me at the street corner. "Hurry up, Rina, or we'll be late," she snaps at me.

"Chill out, Johnny. We won't be late," I answer crossly. It seems like ever since Juanita was kicked out of school for fighting last year and thought she wouldn't graduate, she's become paranoid about school. She's always hurrying us in the morning to make sure we're not tardy, and she never misses a day of school. When we tease Juanita about acting nerdy, she defends herself, saying she won't be stupid like her brother Carlos. He dropped out of school, and ended up working at Burger King.

"Where are the guys?" I finally ask, trying my best to keep up with her as we head in the direction of the school.

"Tyrone's dad let him use the car today, so he and Tommy left real early so they could pick up Maya and

Ankiza. I tried calling you last night, but you weren't home," Juanita says.

"I went to Minerva's," I reply, wondering if Juanita is going to bug me about hanging out with Minerva. I'm sure that Tyrone or Tommy already told her they saw me at the park last night. And I know that Juanita doesn't like Minerva at all because of her bad rep at school. But Juanita doesn't say anything about Minerva. She stays quiet. One thing I like about Juanita, she's not pushy and nosy like Maya.

When we get to campus, Juanita and I go off in separate directions to our lockers. Then I hurry to my first-period class, World History, which I can't stand. Mr. Campton is so boring, all he does is lecture away while everyone in class tunes him out.

By the time I get to my Algebra class, I'm feeling restless and agitated. My head is hurting even more and I don't feel like working math problems. Mrs. Allen beams with pride while Maya, who is one of her star students, finishes a problem on the board. When Mrs. Allen calls out my name, I pretend I don't hear, but she repeats my name insistently. Chuck Martin, who is sitting directly behind me, pokes me in the back, saying, "Can't you hear, stupid?" I can feel everyone in class staring at me. Suddenly, I erupt like a volcano. I turn around and kick Chuck Martin in the leg as hard as I can, calling him every bad word I've ever learned. A look of shock appears on his face, but before he can respond to my insults, Mrs. Allen is standing next to me.

"Rina," she demands in a stern voice, "go to the principal's office. Right now!"

"My pleasure," I answer, storming out of the class-room.

Instead of going to the principal's office, I go to the bathroom, where I hide out until the lunch bell rings. Then I go back to my locker, dump my books and head for the football field to meet my friends for lunch. When I get there, Maya, Juanita and Ankiza are already wait-ing for me. They're sitting on the empty bleachers with Tommy, Tyrone and Rudy, who is Juanita's boyfriend. Everything is pretty cool until Maya opens her big mouth and tells everyone what happened in Algebra. She even repeats a few of the names I threw at Chuck, saying, "Why do you have to be that way, Rina? You know Chuck's a wuss."

"Don't act so prissy, Maya. I was just playing around," I tell her, feeling myself start to boil inside. If there's anything I hate, it's being told how I should act, especially by one of my friends.

At that exact moment, Rudy opens his big mouth and says, "Hey, Maya, didn't you know Rina's always gross. She was born like that!"

Without giving it a moment's thought, I reach across Juanita and punch Rudy in the stomach. Then I stand up and challenge him, "Come on. Get up so I can kick your ass."

Rudy lets out a deep groan, and there is a look of dis-belief on Juanita's face. Tommy is suddenly at my side, pulling me away from Rudy. "Chill out, Rina," he insists. "Rudy was just playing around. You know how he is."

I want to punch Rudy one more time, but Tommy's words convince me to hold back my anger. Still, it's unbelievable to me how Tommy can defend Rudy. After all, Rudy was the one who called Tommy all those bad names when we found out Tommy was gay.

"Yeah, Rina. What's your problem?" Rudy says, glaring at me. "Are you ragging it today?"

As I sit back down next to Ankiza and Maya, I holler at Rudy, "If anyone's on the rag, it's you, *pendejo!*"

Rudy gets up, telling Juanita, "Come on. Let's go. Someone's freaking today." And they take off back to campus alone.

Now everyone is suddenly very quiet, and I can tell they're all wondering why I'm acting like this. What do I care? My life is none of their business. I don't need nothing from nobody.

Four

Rina

When I get home from school, Mom is in the living room watching her favorite Spanish *telenovela* , or soap opera. I right away know that Dad's not home because he hates it when Mom relaxes with her *telenovelas*. Sometimes he'll turn the TV off and order her to fix him something to eat, even if he's not hungry.

"What's for dinner?" I ask, flinging my backpack on the floor so that I can sit next to little Joey, who is busy playing with his G.I. Joe on the edge of the couch.

"Your dad won't be home for dinner. I thought we'd order a pizza," Mom answers cheerfully, keeping her eyes focused on the tall, handsome guy on the screen.

Little Joey shouts, "Yay! I love pizza!" And then he goes back to exploding bombs.

I'm glad Dad won't be home for dinner. We always have fun when he's not here. And besides, Mom gets a day off from cooking. Me, I'd hate to have to cook every day. Once Mom tried to show me how to make this

Puerto Rican dish with fried bananas, but I burned the bananas and complained so much about it that she never asked me to cook again. Mom says I'll make a terrible wife someday, but I tell her I don't want to be anybody's wife. I just want to be me. I don't want to have to wait on a stupid man all my life, like she does for Dad.

"Where's Carmen?" I ask, wondering if Mom wishes she were one of the women in her *telenovelas*, waiting to be rescued by Prince Charming.

"She's next door with her friend. *Ay, m'ija*," Mom sighs, "Román's asking Camila to marry him!"

I stare blankly at the TV screen. The tall handsome Prince Charming is holding out a box with a diamond ring to the sexy brunette whose face is beaming with joy. I want to tell Mom that it's all fake. That it's just a dumb soap opera. That there aren't any Prince Charmings. But she looks so happy, I don't have the heart. Instead, I tell her I'm going upstairs to start my homework.

In my room, I kick off my shoes, turn on the radio and I start my Spanish assignment. Maya always gripes at me and tells me I should do math first, since that's the hardest subject I have. But I don't pay attention to her. Besides, I love Spanish. I've been speaking it since I was a baby. Sometimes I even write poems in Spanish.

I stay in my room until little Joey comes and tells me the pizza has arrived. Then I go downstairs to join Mom, Carmen and little Joey, who are seated in the living room eating pizza. Whenever we order pizza, Mom lets us watch TV while we eat. If Dad knew, he'd have a major heart attack. He always insists that we follow the rules, that we eat at exactly six o'clock, that we don't talk too much at the table and that we finish every last bite on our plates. But when Dad's gone, Mom lets us do things differently. We even get to watch whatever we want on TV.

Tonight, we watch a re-run of *The Cosby Show*, which is Carmen's and Joey's favorite program. When *The Cosby Show* ends, I flip to MTV. Mom frowns when a video comes on with the lyrics, "Do you want to sex me up?" We all start laughing when Carmen gets up and tries to imitate the dance movements of the female singer. Sometimes Carmen can be real funny. Still, most of the time she's a pest.

When it's time for Carmen and Joey to go to bed, I go back upstairs to finish the rest of my homework. In American Lit, we're finishing the novel *Their Eyes Were Watching God* by Zora Neale Hurston. Mrs. Hancock says Zora Neale Hurston was an amazing woman for her time. That she didn't take nothing from nobody. Someday I'd like to be like Zora Neale Hurston.

I'm sound asleep when I hear a loud crash that makes me jerk my head up from the bed. Startled by the sudden noise, the first thing I do is tiptoe over to Carmen's and Joey's room to make sure they're safe. Then, as I head back down the dark hallway, I hear Dad shouting downstairs. My heart starts to pound wildly. A familiar wave of fear overtakes me. I hurry into my room and shut the door behind me. Then I let myself sink to the floor, where I huddle in the dark, hoping to block out the shouting voices. I repeat the verses to a poem in my head over and over until the shouting finally stops. I'm about to crawl into my bed, when I hear Mom's voice outside my door pleading for Dad to let her go, "*Suéltame, José. Por el amor de Dios, suéltame.*"

"This time I'm gonna kill you!" I hear Dad yell.

A shiver passes through my entire body. I'm not sure why I do it, but I jerk open my bedroom door. Even though it's dark, I can make out the cold, hateful expression on Dad's face. He's dragging Mom by the hair toward the bathroom. Mom is struggling hard to free herself from Dad's grasp, but he refuses to let go of her.

"Don't do this, José, *los niños,*" Mom begs, but Dad tells her to shut up as he continues to drag her down the hallway.

I freeze with fear as I see the glint of the kitchen knife in his hand. From somewhere deep down inside, I force every muscle in my body to move, and before Dad can notice me, I step around him to block his path to the bathroom door. "Leave Mom alone," I grumble from deep in my throat.

Dad's eyes are brimming with fire. "Get out of here," he orders me, slipping the knife in his back pocket.

"I won't move from here until you let go of Mom," I shout, my voice quivering with fear.

All of a sudden, Dad releases Mom's hair and steps toward me. The last thing I hear before he swings at me is Mom's frightened voice pleading with Dad to leave me alone.

The blow to my head has me dizzy for a few seconds. When I'm finally able to pull myself up from the floor, I can feel a sharp pain on the right side of my face. Then I'm pounding like crazy on the bathroom door, begging Dad to open it up for me, when I hear little Joey start to cry. I turn around to find him and Carmen standing directly behind me. "Go back to the room with Joey and lock the door behind you," I order Carmen, who does exactly as I tell her.

After I pound on the door a few more times, I realize that Dad's not going to unlock it, so I take off downstairs and dial 911. Choking up inside, I tell them what's happened, all the while praying in my head that the police will arrive quickly. I don't want Mom to die. Within a few minutes, two police officers are at the front door. For once I'm grateful for the police cars that are constantly patrolling the *barrio*.

I follow the two officers upstairs. Once at the bathroom, they force Dad to open up the door. I go into the bedroom with Carmen and little Joey. I'm not sure how much time passes while we lay in bed clinging to each other before one of the officers finally comes looking for us.

"I'm Officer Tim and I wanted to let you know that your mother's out of danger now." Then, with a look of pity on his face, he asks me, "Miss, can I talk to you alone?"

As I step into the hallway with Officer Tim, I'm suddenly ashamed—ashamed for me, for Carmen, for little Joey, for our whole damn family. In a hushed voice, Officer Tim calmly explains to me that Dad has been taken to jail. When I ask about Mom, he tells me she was taken to the Emergency Room because she was bleeding badly from stab wounds. After he reassures me again that Mom's going to be fine, he asks if there are any other family members we can stay with until she gets out of the hospital. In a shaky voice, I give him *Titi* Carmen and *Tío* Victor's phone number.

Half an hour later, *Titi* Carmen comes to pick us up. As she drives us to her apartment, she curses Dad left and right, saying what an idiot her sister is for putting up with him all these years.

"I'm damn tired of rescuing her every time he beats her," she repeats several times. "I don't know how many times I've told Alma that one of these days, José's going to kill her. He's an animal. She needs to kick his butt out and keep him locked up!"

By the time we get to *Titi* Carmen and *Tío* Victor's apartment, which is on the south side of Laguna, little Joey has fallen fast asleep. I carry him into the small living room and lay him down on the sofa-bed which *Titi* Carmen has already fixed up for us. I can tell that Carmen is still scared, because she begs me to sleep next to her, even though she hates sleeping in the middle.

That night, all I do is toss and turn while images of the shiny kitchen knife flash before me. I can't help but hear Mom's screams in my head and I'm instantly filled

with hatred and anger for Dad. But when I think about
him being locked up in jail, I feel guilty and confused.

Five

Rina

Titi Carmen lets us stay home the following day, but on Thursday morning *Tío* Victor, who works as a night watchman at a warehouse, drives us to school. First we take Joey and Carmen to Newman Elementary and then *Tío* Victor drops me off at Roosevelt High. I've always liked *Tío* Victor. He doesn't talk much, but he's always real patient with my little brother and sister. Abuela's always saying what a shame it is that he and *Titi* Carmen can't have kids.

It isn't easy going back to my classes after what has happened. Everyone asks me about my swollen lip. I make up a story about how I crashed when I was giving little Joey a ride on the handle bars of my bike. Most of the kids laugh, but I can tell that my close friends don't believe it.

At lunch time, Rudy runs off at the mouth again and mentions that he saw the cops at my apartment on Wednesday night. When Ankiza asks me what happened, I make up another story, saying that Dad was caught drinking and driving, so the cops took him to jail. Tommy eyes me suspiciously, and Juanita starts to ask me something, but changes her mind in mid-sentence. I'm starting to wonder if I should get up and leave when Maya changes the subject and tells everyone that she's going to spend spring break in the Bay Area with her dad so they can shop for a car. I think about my own dad and how he's locked up behind bars. If Maya only knew how lucky she is to have a dad who's not a psycho like mine. Why is it that I can't have a normal dad like my friends instead of this worthless one I love and hate at the same time?

During the rest of lunch period, I force myself to join in on the conversation with my friends. But as the day wears on, I start to feel more depressed about my life.

After school, I decide to take the city bus to General Hospital. When I walk into Mom's room, she's propped up in bed watching TV. As soon as she sees me, Mom's face lights up with a smile. *"M'ija,* I'm so glad you came," Mom whispers, reaching out for my hand. There are scratches and bruises on her arm. "Are the kids okay?" Mom asks.

I abruptly pull my hand away from hers, saying, "Yeah, I guess so. They like being with *Tío* Victor. But Joey keeps asking for you."

A sad look clouds Mom's dark eyes, and deep furrows appear on her forehead, making her look old and cracked, like the pictures I've seen of the Grand Canyon.

"Tell the kids I'm coming home tomorrow," Mom says, exhaling deeply. "The doctor says I'm healing fine and that he'll take the stitches out next week."

Mom winces as she touches the bulky bandage on the left side of her gown. I'm not sure what I should say next, so I wait in silence. After a very long minute, Mom adds, "This time, I'm filing charges so they can lock him up for good, *m'ija*. You won't have to worry anymore."

I notice the tears in Mom's eyes and I can feel the anger inside of me start to subside. I'm glad Mom has made this decision and that tomorrow we can all go back home. *Titi* Carmen was wrong. Mom isn't so stupid.

"I'll tell Carmen to take the bus home after school tomorrow, and if you want, I can pick up Joey at the babysitter's on my way home."

"Thanks, *m'ija*. I don't know what I'd do without you," Mom says, reaching for me. Only this time I don't pull my hand away. I let her hold it for a long time.

Later that evening, when I tell Carmen and Joey that we're going home tomorrow, they're overjoyed. Little Joey starts to jump up and down, chanting that he's going to play with all his G.I. Joes. And Carmen tells me how much she's missed playing with her friends.

After they go to bed, I tell *Titi* Carmen what Mom said about filing charges against Dad.

"Well, I sure hope she means it this time," she shrugs. "I'm sick of telling her to get rid of the bum. And your Abuela doesn't help much either. She seems to think it's a man's right to do whatever the hell he pleases to his wife."

I want to tell *Titi* Carmen to shut up, that Mom isn't as stupid as everyone thinks, but I don't. After all, she'll soon find out for herself that Mom means business.

After school the next day, instead of walking home with my friends, I go straight to Mrs. Ochoa's house to pick up Joey. Mrs. Ochoa has been Joey's babysitter since he started pre-school. She babysits three other children besides her own two, who are still in diapers. I always think that Mrs. Ochoa must have nerves of steel to watch that many bratty kids. Me, I'm never gonna have kids.

Mrs. Ochoa's house is about a ten minute walk from Roosevelt. When I get there, Joey is in the front yard playing with Ricky, who is a few years younger.

"Hey, monster. Time to go," I announce as I open the gate and head up the small walkway.

A big smile appears on Joey's face when he sees me. He drops the Batman motorcycle he's playing with and races inside for his backpack. Mrs. Ochoa comes to the door. She's balancing her six-month-old baby in one arm while she holds on to four-year-old Jenny.

"Hi, Rina," Mrs. Ochoa says. "Joey's been excited all afternoon about going home." Then she goes on to ask, "Is your mom gonna be all right?"

"She's fine," I answer, ignoring the look of pity on Mrs. Ochoa's face. Then little Joey comes out and I thank Mrs. Ochoa as I take him by the hand. I'm not sure what Mom told Mrs. Ochoa. Most of the time, she lies to cover up for my dad.

As soon as little Joey opens the front door to our apartment, he screams, "Yeah, Daddy's home!" Then he runs over to Dad, who is sitting on the couch watching TV.

I'm in shock. Something's not right, I tell myself, breaking out in a cold sweat. When I'm finally able to speak, I ask rudely, "Where's Mom?"

Carmen, who has been sitting at the bottom of the stairs watching me, says, "Mom's upstairs, resting."

I hear Dad ask me about school, but I don't answer him. I rush upstairs, feeling the anger mounting up inside of me. When I walk into Mom's room, I explode into a thousand pieces, "I thought you weren't letting him come back!" I yell defiantly.

Embarrassed, Mom's eyes start to fill with tears, but I don't care. The only thing I care about is that she has lied to me.

"I couldn't do it, m'ija," Mom explains. "He came to see me at the hospital and he begged me not to. He said he's going to change, get counseling. He promised it'll never happen again."

I don't believe what I've just heard. I'm so mad that I can feel my knees start to get wobbly. I want to slap Mom, shake her until she rolls to the floor like a little rag doll. "*Titi* Carmen was right. You are stupid!" I shout at her. "I hate you and I hate Dad too!"

Mom tries to reason with me, but I'm too upset to listen. "Well, if you want to keep on taking this, go ahead. But I don't. I can't stand it any more. I'm leaving. And I'm taking little Joey and Carmen with me!"

Mom begs me to come back as I turn around, slamming the door behind me. When I look up, Dad is standing at the end of the hallway with Joey. I can tell by the mean look on his face that he's heard every single word I've said.

"José and Carmen aren't going anywhere. They're staying right here with me," Dad warns me.

Little Joey looks as if he's about to cry and, for a brief moment, I think about yanking him away from Dad. But I'm too frightened to do it. I know that the only way I'll leave this house is without Joey and Carmen. Instead, I flee to my room, where I nervously throw some things into my duffel bag.

When I go back downstairs, Joey is outside with Dad in the back patio. As I get ready to leave out the front door, Carmen comes over and hands me a small box.

"Here's some money I've saved. Maybe you'll need it," she whispers, teary-eyed.

I stuff the small box into my backpack. Then I reach down and hug Carmen, telling her, "Take care of Joey."

I head for downtown, unsure of where I should go. I think about going back to *Titi* Carmen's, but I know that I can't face her. After all, she was dead right about Mom. Finally, I make up my mind to take the bus to Abuela's house. As soon as Abuela opens the door, she says, *"¿Qué te pasa, hija?* What are you doing here at this hour?" I tell Abuela everything that's happened, explaining that I've come to live with her. Abuela nods her head, muttering under her breath, *"Es la culpa de tu mamá* . If she'd only mind what José tells her to do, they wouldn't have these problems."

Six

Ms. Martínez

I was just about to complete the summary from my final counseling session of the day, when I was interrupted by a light knocking on my office door. "Darn," I muttered to myself, hoping it wasn't a drop-in client. I had promised Frank I'd try to get home early this evening so we could have a normal, sit-down dinner. For the past few weeks, given Frank's income tax work and my erratic schedule, all we'd been eating were microwaved meals and fast food. Not that Frank was complaining. He loved fast food. Frank could live on hamburgers and french fries and Taco Bell tacos. You'd think he was still in college.

When I opened the door, I was surprised to find Tommy and Maya waiting in the hallway. Although she seemed a bit uncomfortable, Maya was the first to speak.

"Hi, Ms. Martínez. We thought we'd check up on you to see how the shrink business is going."

"How sweet of you," I said, smiling and inviting them inside my office.

As Tommy and Maya took a seat on the couch across from my desk, I wondered what in the world they could possibly want. It had been quite a while since I'd visited with both of them at the same time.

"How's school?" I asked, hoping this question would bring out the reason for their unexpected visit.

Maya began to talk excitedly about spring break and how she would be visiting her dad in San Francisco so that they could shop around for her first car. When Tommy teased Maya about being rich and spoiled, she poked him with her skinny elbow, saying, "Don't be a wuss, Tommy."

Tommy's handsome face lit up with a smile as he kicked Maya playfully with his sneaker, telling her, "Speak for yourself!"

I thought back to Tommy's suicide attempt and the rejections he had received from his parents and friends when they had found out he was gay. Maya had defended Tommy and stood by his side throughout the entire ordeal. It was good to know that they continued to be the best of friends.

Maya proceeded to nudge Tommy again with her elbow saying, "*Andale*, Tommy, tell Ms. Martínez why we're here."

Tommy hesitated nervously for a moment before he began his explanation. "We came to ask for your help, Ms. Martínez. It's about our friend Rina. Rina Morales. She hasn't been in school for a week and—"

"We think something bad's happened to Rina," Maya interrupted. "We think it has to do with her step-dad. But we're afraid to go to Rina's apartment and ask for her. You see, Rina thinks we don't know, but her dad beats on her mom all the time."

"Yeah, Ms. Martínez," Tommy interjected. "Last week Rina came to school with a busted lip, and when we asked her what happened, she lied about it. We all knew it had something to do with her dad 'cause the police were at her house the night before. Rina lives in the same apartments as I do, and my mom's *comadre* told her they saw the ambulance take Rina's mom away."

All of a sudden, I was starting to get a sick feeling in my stomach.

Maya leaned forward, staring at me with worried-looking eyes. "We don't know what to think, Ms. Martínez, 'cause ever since that day at school when we asked Rina about her busted lip, she hasn't come to school."

While I sifted through the information Tommy and Maya had just given me, I racked my brain trying to remember if I'd ever met Rina. Then it dawned on me why this name sounded so familiar. Rina was the Puerto Rican friend who had witnessed Juanita's fight at school with Sheena several years ago.

"Do you think you can help us, Ms. Martínez?" Maya asked, bringing me back to the present.

"All I can do is try. Why don't you tell me where Rina lives, and I'll stop in on my way home to see if I can find out anything."

"Thanks, Ms. Martínez," Maya sighed.

As Tommy wrote down Rina's apartment number, he cautioned me, "But watch out, Ms. Martínez, 'cause Rina's dad is real mean."

"Don't worry about me," I quickly responded with a teasing smile. "Us shrinks are invincible!"

"Yeah, right," Maya said, and we all started to laugh.

✎ ✐ ✎

It took me less than five minutes to get from my office to the dirty brown apartment complex where most of Laguna's poor residents lived. A few Anglo families occupied the government-subsidized housing project, but the majority of the tenants were people of color. It never ceased to amaze me how a wealthy university city like Laguna could have so many poor people working as busboys, cooks and motel maids.

After a few light knocks, the door to Rina's apartment was half-opened, and I found myself being scrutinized by a young girl with the biggest eyes I'd ever seen.

"Hello," I greeted the pretty little girl. "Is your mother home?"

The young girl spun around quickly to call out, *"Mami, it's for you!"*

A few seconds later, a tall dark lady peered at me through the open doorway. There was a bruise right below her right eye.

"Hello. You must be Mrs. Morales. My name is Sandra Martínez, Dr. Sandra Martínez," I said, pausing. Mrs. Morales continued to stare at me blankly, so I decided to get right to the point. "I was hoping to speak with you about your daughter, Rina. I understand that she hasn't been in school for a week."

Mrs. Morales exhaled deeply. Just as she was about to say something, the door was flung wide open and a handsome Latino who reminded me of my grandfather when he was in his early thirties, appeared at her side. "Alma," he scolded, "have you forgotten your manners? Please come in," he insisted.

As I stepped inside the small living room, he held his hand out to me me saying, "I'm José, José Morales, and this is my wife, Alma. "

To be polite, I shook Mr. Morales' hand and introduced myself again. As I sat down on an armchair next to the TV, I noticed a young boy sitting on the floor watching cartoons. Before I could say hello to him, Mr. Morales ordered Carmen in Spanish to take the young boy upstairs to play. Carmen quickly obeyed, pulling her little brother to his feet and forcing him away from the TV despite his complaints.

As soon as they were out of the room, Mr. Morales flashed me a big smile and said, "Now, what can we do for you?"

"As I was telling your wife, some of your daughter's friends came to see me today in my office. I'm a psychologist here in town, and well, to put it bluntly, they're very concerned because Rina hasn't been in school. Has Rina been ill?" Out of the corner of my eye, I observed Mrs. Morales. She appeared to be very nervous. She kept her eyes lowered and avoided looking directly at me.

"No, no, Rina's fine," Mr. Morales explained, revealing a row of yellowish brown teeth that made him look years older. Probably a chain smoker, I thought to myself.

"You see, her grandmother, *Doña* Martina, got sick, and Rina went to help take care of her. That's why she hasn't been in school."

Mrs. Morales glanced up at me as if she wanted to say something else, but Mr. Morales put his hand on her arm and said, "Right, *vieja*?"

I watched as they exchanged a quick, intense look. Mrs. Morales finally nodded, silently agreeing with her husband.

"I'm glad Rina isn't ill," I said, hoping to sound convincing. Judging by Mrs. Morales' guarded behavior, I could tell that something wasn't quite right. "Do you think you might be able to give me her grandmother's address and phone number?" I added.

"*¡Cómo no! Andale, vieja*. Get the address for this nice lady," Mr. Morales replied, ordering his wife to get him a paper and pencil.

A minute later, Mr. Morales handed me the address saying, "We'll make sure Rina goes to school next week. Right, *vieja*?"

Once more, Mrs. Morales nodded silently.

As I stood up to leave, Mr. Morales asked me if I was from Mexico, telling me that I looked like a *mexicana*. Then he proudly informed me that he was from a small *rancho* in Michoacán.

Mrs. Morales remained silent.

Seven

Ms. Martínez

As I drove to the south side of Laguna, I kept thinking about my conversation with José Morales. It was clear from the way he treated Rina's mom that he was very controlling. He was obviously trying to put up a front, make it seem as if things were fine with Rina, with all of them. All lies, of that I was sure. After all, if anyone knew what it was like to grow up surrounded by lies, it was me. All those teenage years trying to avoid the truth about my father's drinking, making up stories every time Dad had an accident. I recognized all too well the fear in Mrs. Morales' eyes.

As I parked my car in front of the duplex where Rina's grandmother lived, I remembered that years ago I had given one of my clients a ride home to this very same neighborhood. It was a nice area, a few blocks from the YMCA, which included a large park with a new baseball field. A string of new apartments were going up around the old duplexes that had been here for many years.

Just as soon as I rang the doorbell, the door was opened by a stout elderly lady with piercing brown eyes. "Hello," I said, holding out my hand to her. "You must be *Doña* Martina. My name is Sandra Martínez."

With a puzzled look on her face, *Doña* Martina politely greeted me.

"I'm a counselor, and it's come to my attention that Rina hasn't been attending school."

Doña Martina, who appeared to be healthy as a horse, turned around and shouted, *"Rina, ven acá."* Then she invited me into the living room, where I promptly sat down on the couch. I stared at the family pictures on the walls while *Doña* Martina nervously explained that someone else from the high school had called yesterday asking why Rina wasn't in school. Just then, Rina walked into the room. The resemblance to her mother was striking. Rina was tall and big-boned with the same dark skin and big eyes as her mother.

"Hello, Rina. I'm Ms. Martínez," I said cheerfully, holding out my hand to her. Rina hesitated before she finally walked over to shake my hand and take a seat on the far end of the couch. *Doña* Martina excused herself and disappeared into the kitchen for some coffee.

Hoping to break Rina's silence, I pointed to an 8x10 picture on top of the TV of a young girl. "That's a nice picture. Is that you?" I asked.

"Yeah, I look real dorky," Rina answered as *Doña* Martina reappeared with coffee and a plate full of cookies. Not wanting to seem rude, I helped myself to a cup of coffee and some cookies, telling *Doña* Martina that I had been to San Juan, Puerto Rico, on several occasions.

Doña Martina was pleased and she began to talk about how she was born and raised in San Juan. I chatted with her for a few minutes about my visit to old San Juan and how impressed I had been by its history and architectural beauty. Rina sat listening quietly while she ate one cookie after another.

After a few minutes, *Doña* Martina excused herself once more, saying that she knew I had come to talk to Rina. As soon as she left the room, I said, "Rina, I've come to talk to you about school. Some of your friends are very concerned because you haven't been to school for a week."

"What friends?" Rina asked rudely.

"Tommy and Maya. They're very worried about you. They asked me if I would go to your apartment to find out if anything was wrong, which I did. Your dad told me you were here helping your grandma, who was ill. Is that true?"

A sarcastic laugh escaped from Rina's lips as she started to fidget with her fingernails.

"Is that the reason why you haven't been in school?" I repeated, hoping to extract some sort of explanation from her. Out of the corner of my eye, I noticed that *Doña* Martina was standing in the doorway to the kitchen, listening to our conversation.

"Yeah, sure," Rina stammered, breaking one of her long nails.

"Well, your grandma seems fine now. When do you think you'll be able to get back to school?"

"I'm not sure," Rina hesitated.

"I'd like to help in any way I can," I continued despite Rina's detachment. "I can contact the school if you'd like or I can try talking to your parents again."

Rina was suddenly on her feet. "No! I don't need anybody's help," she yelled at me defiantly. "You tell everyone to stay out of my business!"

Then Rina stormed out of the room before I had time to say anything else. *Doña* Martina came back into the room, apologizing for her granddaughter's behavior. *"Maleducada,"* she mumbled under her breath. "Just like her mother."

Doña Martina's attitude warned me that it would be useless trying to get any helpful information from her about Rina's family situation. I stood up, saying it was time for me to leave. As she walked me to the door, I thanked *Doña* Martina for her hospitality and handed her my business card so that she could give it to Rina.

✎ ⬒ ✐

By the time I pulled into the driveway, it was already dark. I hurried out of the car and into the house, where I found Frank sitting on the couch watching the Comedy Channel. "Hi, gorgeous," he said, lowering the volume on the TV.

"Sorry I'm late," I apologized, setting my briefcase on the floor and walking over to Frank to give him a warm kiss on the mouth.

"Mmmm, got any more of that?" Frank teased, his sea-blue eyes sparkling mischieviously.

I smiled as I sat down next to him and kicked off my blue pumps.

"Now don't worry, hon. I've got everything under control. Our *fajita* TV dinners will be ready in a half hour."

"Oh, good. I'm too tired to cook," I sighed, running my hand through Frank's curly blonde hair.

"Bad day at the shrinkmobile?"

"Not really. Everything went smoothly until Tommy and Maya showed up."

"Uh-oh, here you go again. Trying to save all the kids in the world. What happened now?"

Frank listened attentively while I described my brief encounter with Mr. and Mrs. Morales and my subsequent visit with Rina. When I ended, Frank asked, "Do you really think Mr. Morales beats his wife?"

"Well, I can't be sure yet, but the bruises on her face certainly point to domestic violence. And all the signs are there. It's obvious Mrs. Morales is afraid of her husband. She wouldn't speak unless he allowed her to. I was hoping Rina would open up to me, but she didn't. She's very explosive, angry."

"Did the grandmother say anything at all?"

"No, nothing really. I have a feeling she's in denial herself. It's all so depressing, yet typical. Do you know that every thirteen seconds in the United States an incidence of violence occurs against a woman by her partner? More than four million women are battered by their partners each year."

"Those are disturbing statistics," Frank said.

"And most kids who witness abusive behavior in their families will carry domestic violence into their own homes at some point in their lives."

Frank was silent for a moment or two. "So is there anything you can do to help Rina and her mother?"

"I'm not sure. At this point, there isn't much I can do unless they're both willing to ask for my help."

The timer on the oven suddenly went off and we were both relieved for an excuse to break away from the depressing topic of conversation. While I set the table for dinner, Frank took the *fajita* dinners out of the oven. I was about to reach for my usual can of Pepsi when Frank asked me to heat him up a couple of *tortillas*. After a quick search in the refrigerator, I turned to him, explaining that we were completely out of *tortillas*.

"What? There's no *tortillas*?" Frank exclaimed, breaking into a loud rendition of Lalo Guerrero's popular song:

> "There's no *tortillas*.
> There's only bread.
> There's no *tortillas*.
> And I feel so sad.
> My grief I can not hide.
> There's no *tortillas*
> for my refrieds."

By the time Frank ended the song, I was laughing hysterically.

Eight

Rina

By Friday, I'm about ready to explode from listening to Abuela's complaints. It seems like ever since Ms. Martínez came to the house, all Abuela does is nag me about going back to school. Then she starts griping about Mom, saying that if Mom were a good wife, bad things wouldn't happen to her. I can't take it anymore, so that evening I decide to call Minerva. She tells me to be at City Park by seven, that Charley has invited us to a big party that some of his friends are having at Seaside Beach. Abuela eyes me suspiciously when I tell her that I'm going to a friend's house to watch a movie. But for once, she doesn't ask me any questions.

By the time the bus drops me off at City Park, it's almost seven-thirty. I head straight for Charley's car, which is parked by the bathrooms. When I get there, Minerva and Charley are sitting on top of a picnic table, smoking a cigarette. Minerva is wearing a brown leather jacket with long tassels on it, which makes her look like a hippie.

"What took you so long?" she asks as I approach them.

"Sorry I'm late. The bus was real slow."

"Don't sweat it, *esa*," Charley says, flicking the remainder of his cigarette on the grass. Then he announces that we'd better leave before they run out of booze at the party. If you ask me, all Charley thinks about is getting high.

It only takes us fifteen minutes to drive to Seaside. It's a small beach city north of Laguna. I'd never been there before, but I heard it's where a lot of the teenagers and college kids party on weekends. Charley drives around until he spots his friend Mike's car at one of the secluded beaches on the north side. Then we hurry out of the car toward the beach to join a large group of kids who are gathered around a big bonfire. The music coming from the beach party drowns out the fierce ocean waves.

As we approach the group, I recognize some of Charley's friend's I met once before at City Park. Charley starts talking to his pimple-faced friend Mike, who immediately offers him a beer. When Minerva says, "Hey, what about us?" Mike is forced to hand each of us a can of beer.

Minerva and I sit on a blanket next to this guy and girl whose names we don't even know, but it doesn't seem to bother them, 'cause they're too busy making out. As I look around, I notice several other couples making out, but no one seems to mind, so I try not to let it get to me.

After a couple of beers, I'm getting a buzz. Charley is still talking to Mike, and Minerva is dancing with a weird-looking guy with a shaved head. The couple next to me gets up to join them, and soon a bunch of people are dancing. I start to joke around with Mark Alderson, who is from my Math class. He introduces me to his friend, Juan, who looks like he's pretty smashed. When Juan tries to put his arm around my waist, I shove his arm away and wave my fist angrily in his face.

"Get away from me, you dog!" I'm about to punch him when Minerva comes up and says, "Come on, Rina, chill out."

Juan gets up and with a slurred voice, tells Mark, "Come on. She's all freaked out," and they leave to join some other friends.

"Here, have another one on me," Minerva says, handing me another beer before she takes off to dance again. I'm about to take a long swig when I hear someone call my name. I turn to find Maya, Tyrone and Tommy standing a few feet away from me. I start to get up and I lose my balance slightly, but I manage to regain control as they walk up to me.

"You're wasted, Rina," Maya says, grabbing hold of my arm like a sister.

"Just having a good time, that's all," I say, waving my can in the air.

Tyrone gives me a look of disgust as he walks over to the bonfire to talk with someone else.

"Rina, I think you should go home now," Tommy snaps. "You can barely stand up."

I laugh sarcastically, taking a long drink just to spite them both. But the next thing I know, everything is spinning around me and I feel like I'm floating on the sand. "I think I need to puke," I suddenly moan, covering my mouth with my hand.

Maya tells Tommy to go get Tyrone as she takes me away from the crowd. I can feel the cramps getting stronger as we walk toward the bathrooms. We're almost there when I have to stop to throw up. After I'm finished, Maya hands me a Kleenex to wipe my mouth.

"Are you feeling better?" she asks. I nod, wondering why I drank so much beer when I don't even like how it tastes.

Just then Tommy and Tyrone come walking up to us. "We told Minerva you're going home with us, Rina," Tyrone tells me in a stern voice.

"Yeah, but we need to sober you up before we take you home," Tommy adds.

I'm feeling too weak to argue with anyone, so I let Maya take me by the arm and lead me to Tommy's car. I climb into the front seat next to Tommy while Tyrone and Maya sit in the back. As we drive away, Tommy says, "That was a stupid thing to do, Rina."

"Yeah, right, you oughta know," I repeat indignantly. Tommy doesn't say anything, but I can tell that I've hurt his feelings. Who the heck does he think he is to lecture me about drinking anyway? It was only a few months ago that he had a rep for going to school drunk.

"Don't be a smartass, Rina," Tyrone scolds me from the back seat, but Maya quickly tells him to cool it.

Back in Laguna, we drive to Foster Freeze, where they pump coffee into me until I begin to feel more alert. My head is still throbbing and my mouth is dry, but at least I'm not dizzy any more.

When Maya feels that I've sobered up enough, she tells Tommy that it's time for him to take her home. We drop Maya off at her house first. Then we go back to the *barrio* and leave Tyrone at his apartment. As we drive past Mom's apartment, I notice that the lights are still on. A deep sadness penetrates my heart as I think about Carmen and little Joey. Tommy glances at me and he catches me wiping a tear that has escaped from the corner of my eye, but he doesn't say anything. We drive in silence, until we get to Abuela's house. Then Tommy turns to me and says, "Come on, Rina! Why won't you tell me what's going on? Don't you know by now that I'm your friend?"

I don't know exactly what to say to Tommy. But suddenly I am ashamed for having been rude to him earlier. After all, Tommy has had his share of problems. A lot of kids still talk about him behind his back, calling him bad names.

"You can trust me, Rina," Tommy goes on. "I know what it's like to feel all alone, like no one gives a damn."

I look deeply into Tommy's eyes, sensing all of his grief, and before I even realize what's happening, I tell him about the night Dad almost killed Mom, about how

I ran away to Abuela's 'cause I'm sick of seeing Dad beat on Mom, that I can't live like that any more.

When the tears begin to flow, Tommy slides next to me and embraces me until I can't cry anymore. Then, in a calming voice, he says, "Rina, I know Ms. Martínez offered to help you. Won't you please let her? If it weren't for her help, I wouldn't be here."

I turn away from Tommy and I gaze mindlessly at the brightly lit street. But all I can see is the terror in Mom's eyes.

"You'll like her. And I know she can help you. I'll even go with you to her office if you want," Tommy offers.

Inside my head, I can still hear Mom's pleading voice. I can still feel Dad's fist on my face. And from somewhere far away, I hear myself whisper, "Okay, Tommy, I'll go see her."

Nine

Ms. Martínez

Tommy's phone call on Sunday evening had taken me by complete surprise. Unsure of why Tommy was calling me at home and so late at night, I began by asking how he was doing in school. Tommy told me that he was doing great and was looking forward to graduation next year. When I asked if his relationship with his father had improved, Tommy sarcastically replied that he didn't think his macho dad would ever accept having a son who was gay. I reminded Tommy to be patient, and he reluctantly agreed, saying that at least he knew his mom was on his side.

At last, Tommy revealed his reason for calling. He described the beach incident on Saturday night and how he had finally convinced Rina to come and talk with me. Before we hung up, I told Tommy that I would be more than happy to see Rina in my office on Tuesday.

✎ ✐ ✎

At the sound of the buzzer in the reception desk, I hurried out to the waiting room of the old Victorian house where my office was located. Tommy greeted me cheerfully. Then he turned to Rina, who was standing nervously at his side, and he told her he'd be back in an hour. In a loud panicky voice, Rina warned Tommy that if he wasn't back soon, she'd hitchhike home. Tommy laughed as he headed out the front door. Then Rina turned to me and said, "Okay, Doc, where to?"

"Follow me, young lady," I commanded, leading Rina through the hallway and into my office, which was situated in the back next to the kitchen.

Instead of taking a seat, Rina paced anxiously around the room, scrutinizing every object there, from the Frida Kahlo altar Frank had given me on my birthday to the posters on the wall.

"Are you familiar with that group?" I asked Rina, pointing to the "Lighter Shade of Brown" poster Maya had given me last year. Music was always a popular topic of conversation with teens.

"Yeah, they're awesome," Rina replied, finally letting her large, awkward body slump into a corner of the couch.

"I think this is a really stupid idea," she suddenly blurted out. "I don't even know why I'm here."

It was clear to me that Rina was not the quiet introverted type, but rather someone who always said what was on her mind. "What makes you say that?" I asked cautiously.

"Only *locos* talk to shrinks!" Rina answered, looking out the small window next to her. "Who lives back there?" she asked, pointing to the small cottage behind our offices.

Amused by Rina's question, I explained that Mr. Caldwell, the elderly man who was the caretaker for the grounds, lived there by himself.

"Lucky man. Wish I could live all alone," Rina repeated.

"And why would you want to live all alone?" I asked, staring into her beautiful dark eyes.

"I don't know. I guess so no one would bother me."

I was about to say something when Rina suddenly got to her feet and said, "I better go. This was a dumb idea."

Realizing that I needed to think fast before Rina fled from my sight, I thrust a candy dish filled with chocolate kisses at her. "Here, have some candy," I said, remembering how she had sat there quietly and stuffed herself with cookies at her grandma's.

Rina's eyes softened. "I love chocolate kisses," she said, reaching for a handful.

"Rina, please stay a while," I pleaded gently. "I'd really like to get to know you."

Rina hesitated for a moment and then sat back down on the couch and proceeded to eat the candy.

"I can see you're a chocoholic like me," I said.

"Yeah, I guess, but I wish I was skinny like you. I'm a fat cow."

"No, you're not," I quickly defended her. "I see a beautiful young lady sitting in front of me."

Embarrassed, Rina turned away from me. Silence set in as she stared at the single bluebird resting on the tree outside my window. At last, Rina looked at me with tear-filled eyes and said, "I hate my parents. I hate them so bad. But I hate my mom the most."

"What makes you feel that way, Rina?" I asked, leaning slightly forward in my chair.

"They're both stupid. They think I'm blind, that I don't know my dad beats on my mom. And she's so damn stupid, letting him do it."

Tears were rolling down Rina's round cheeks. "I hate them," she repeated, and her body began to shake from the sobs that were now taking possession of her.

I moved to Rina's side, handing her a box of Kleenex. When the tears finally subsided, Rina went on. "That's why I went to live with my Abuela, Ms. Martínez. I couldn't take it anymore. They think I don't know what's been going on all these years. But I've seen it all." Rina paused for a few moments and then, in a shaky voice, she continued. "When I was a little girl, I used to hide under the table and watch. Sometimes I'd even take Joey and Carmen with me and we'd hide and wait until it was all over."

"Wasn't there anyone in your family you could go to for help?" I asked gently.

"Are you kidding?" Rina exclaimed. "Dad would've beat us up if we'd told anyone. The only one who ever knew anything was *Titi* Carmen, mom's sister. She used to come and pick us up late at night after Dad had passed out. *Titi* Carmen was always rescuing us, but she got tired of trying to help us."

I waited patiently while Rina wiped the tears from her stormy eyes and, after a very long minute, she continued.

"I remember it all, Ms. Martínez. Mom thinks I never saw any of it. At first, Dad used to just yell and scream at her, but then he started to hit her. That time he hit her with the pan on the eye, I got so scared. There was blood gushing all over. I wanted to get up to help her, but I was too scared, so I just hid there under the table. Dad was so mad that he made Mom wipe up all the blood herself. After they went to bed, I laid awake all night wondering what he was gonna do to her next. Then around four in the morning, Mom rushed into my room and woke me up. She told me to be real quiet and to help her get Joey and Carmen dressed 'cause we were going to *Titi* Carmen's house. *Titi* Carmen came and picked us up in the alley and we drove straight to the hospital. Mom needed six stitches. She told *Titi* Carmen she had fallen down the stairs, but *Titi* Carmen knew it was all a lie. After that night, I was always afraid. And I hated Mom more for being so stupid. Why, Ms. Martínez? Why does she let Dad beat on her like that?"

Rina's grief-stricken eyes pierced deep into my heart as she searched for an answer to help ease the hurt feelings she had been experiencing for all these years.

"I can't answer for your mom, Rina," I began slowly. "But what I can tell you is that it's not as simple as everyone assumes it is. It's not just a question of the woman getting up and leaving. There are many reasons why a woman stays with a batterer, and the longer she stays with him, the harder it is to get out. The woman becomes weaker and weaker until she is too battered to get out."

"I don't understand why Dad does it," Rina said. "And I hate him so much for it. But I love him, too."

Rina started to cry again, and I put my arm around her, holding her tightly until she had released all her tears. Then I told her, "Rina, I'd very much like to help you. I know you're feeling hurt and angry, and I'd like to try to help you."

Rina stared at me and in a defensive voice, said, "How would you know how bad I feel, Ms. Martínez? All I do is pretend. No one knows how I feel. Not even my friends. I lie to everyone. We all lie in my family."

I reached over and placed Rina's hand in mine. "Rina, this is something I never talk about with anyone except my husband, Frank, but I grew up in an abusive family, like you."

Now I had Rina's complete attention as she waited for me to explain. "You see, my own father is an alcoholic. And I grew up with a lot of verbal abuse, and sometimes he hit my mom. And I was always scared like you."

"Did you tell lies like me so your friends wouldn't find out?"

I nodded. "Yes, we all lied to cover up the truth, hoping to avoid the gossip. But it didn't quite work like that."

Rina was silent again while the room filled with the distant humming of a lawnmower. At last, she turned to me and said, "Okay, Ms. Martínez. I'll let you help me if you think you can."

"Good girl," I said, letting go of her hand and moving back to my desk. "But first things first. With your permission, I'd like to call the high school and see about getting you re-admitted. Is that all right with you?"

A half-smile appeared on Rina's face. "Yeah, Tommy said if I didn't go to school tomorrow, he was gonna come and drag me over there."

"Knowing Tommy, he'll do just that," I said, smiling.

Rina straightened out her wide shoulders, saying, "Nah, he knows I can beat him up and all the guys put together at school."

"Aha! I guess we'll have to call you Rina Schwarzenegger!"

A big smile spread across Rina's beautiful dark face.

"Here, have some more chocolate kisses," I said, smiling back at Rina.

Ten

Ms. Martínez

As soon as Rina left, I dialed Roosevelt High School, and they put me through to Mr. Belchor, the 11th grade counselor. I couldn't help but smile to myself, imagining all the jokes the students must make about his name. Mr. Belchor was sympathetic, reassuring me that a note from Rina's grandmother indicating that there had been a family emergency would allow her back in school. He also said he would contact each of Rina's teachers and explain that she would need make-up assignments. By the time we hung up, I felt pleased, knowing that Mr. Belchor would be watching out for Rina. Next, I called *Doña* Martina to let her know that everything was set for Rina to go back to school, but that she would need a written excuse. *Doña* Martina agreed, and thanked me several times for helping Rina.

Before I left my office, I called Frank to let him know that I was running late. I couldn't help but smile to myself when Frank told me not to worry about dinner, that he would order Chinese take-out and have it there when I arrived. Frank loved to find an excuse to order Chinese food.

Twenty minutes later when I walked through the front door, Frank was sitting in front of the TV pigging out. There were several containers on the coffee table.

"Mmm, it smells delicious," I said, taking off my jacket. Suddenly, I was very hungry.

"Sorry, hon, I couldn't wait any longer," Frank apologized, clumsily taking another mouthful of Kung Pao chicken with his chopsticks.

I gave him a light kiss as he handed me a plate. "I'm starved," I said, helping myself to some shrimp fried rice.

"Oh, before I forget. There was a message on the machine for you from your mother. She wants you to call her. She sounded worried."

"Shoot," I mumbled, feeling a tightening in the back of my neck. I knew that it had to be important for mom to leave a message on the recorder, because she hated answering machines almost as much as Frank did. "I guess I should call her," I sighed, taking a few more bites.

"Sandy, finish eating and then call," Frank insisted. He knew my mother's phone calls tended to upset me.

"You're right," I agreed, helping myself to some more shrimp fried rice.

When we finished eating, Frank turned the Comedy Channel on and we watched Dana Carvey doing his impression of former President George Bush. Frank and I both laughed and I felt the day's tension slowly leave my body. I was just about to lay my head on Frank's lap, when the phone rang. "I'll get it," I reluctantly told Frank.

I hurried into the kitchen and picked up the receiver just as the recorded message was about to end. "Hello."

"Sandra, is that you?" Mom asked in a shrill voice. "Why haven't you called me?"

It was just like Mom to cross-examine me and make me feel like an irresponsible teenager. "Sorry, Mom. I worked late tonight." Why was it I still had to apologize to my mother for everything I did or didn't do?

"It's your dad, Sandra. He's in the hospital. He started bleeding internally this afternoon and it wouldn't stop, so I had to drive him to the emergency room."

My mind suddenly went blank and I felt the tension in my neck start to resurface. "Is he going to be all right?" I asked, reaching up to massage the back of my neck with my left hand.

"The doctor says he thinks the bleeding stopped. They have the tube down his esophagus. Can you come home for a few days?"

Dad's swollen red face flashed before me as I remembered the last time he had started bleeding. It was the day before Thanksgiving. I had been forced to cancel our Thanksgiving plans so that I could drive to Delano to see him. Mom and I had spent the entire night at the hospital at his side until he was out of danger. When he finally came home, Dad swore he'd never drink again. I tried hard to convince him to go to a treatment program nearby, but he wouldn't hear of it, insisting he could do it all on his own. And Mom hadn't helped much either; she

completely denied there was a problem. Frustrated, I had
gone back home to Laguna. Six months later, Dad was
drinking again. Lying. Hiding beer in the garage.

"I don't think I can go, Mom. You know how busy I
am," I replied sharply, hoping she'd get the hint.

"Andale, hija. You know how it cheers him up when
you and Frank visit."

Damn her, I thought to myself. Why couldn't she
understand how much it hurt me to see him this way? Did
she think I was made of stone? And why in the world
would I even think of dropping everything just to go out
there and listen to his lies again? No. I couldn't stand it any
more. If she wanted to continue denying that Dad had a
serious problem, then she could go right ahead and do so
all by herself. I refused to be a part of it anymore.

"I have to go, Mom," I interrupted. "I'll call tomorrow
to see how Dad's doing."

I slammed the receiver down before she had time to
plead any further. Then I went back to join Frank in the
living room.

"What's wrong, hon?" Frank asked as soon as he saw
the strained look on my face.

I started to tell Frank about my conversation with my
mother, and before I knew it, I was crying. Frank pulled
me into his arms and held me until I was feeling better.
When I told Frank how fed up I was with my parents, he
reassured me that I had made the right decision about not
running to my father's side. Then he reminded me of what
I already knew too well: No one could help my father

except himself. I sadly agreed, knowing that Frank was absolutely right.

That night in bed, I thought about Rina and her family. I remembered how I'd tried to protect my younger brother, Andy, just like Rina had tried to do with Joey and Carmen. But I couldn't save him, and he had taken his own life. But I promised myself that I would do everything in my power to help Rina so that she wouldn't end up consumed by the same anger and shame that had destroyed my brother Andy.

Eleven

Rina

The first day back at school, Mr. Belchor calls me into his office to ask me if there's anything I'd like to talk about with him. I stubbornly tell him "no," but Mr. Belchor doesn't let this bother him. Before I leave, he reminds me that if I ever want to talk about my classes or anything else, that I should come see him. It's weird, but until now, I never thought any of the teachers or counselors at Roosevelt cared about me. Maybe I was wrong.

During my first two classes, I manage to push my problems to a dark corner in the back of my mind where they can't hurt me. But when I get to my American Lit class, everything changes. Mrs. Hancock hands out copies of *The Scarlet Letter*, saying that this is one of the most important novels we'll be discussing this semester. When Tim Michaels, one of the biggest whiners in the class, asks, "What's so great about this book?" Mrs. Hancock explains that among other things this novel describes the mistreatment of women in the nineteenth century. It's about a woman who is trapped—trapped in a bad marriage and trapped by society. Tim smiles sarcastically and says, "So what?" Mrs. Hancock goes on to explain how we can learn a great deal by comparing the role of women in earlier times to the role of women today.

I'm instantly reminded of Mom, and I don't know what gets into me, but I fling the novel across the room toward the wastebasket.

Tim and a few other jerks in the class start to clap and holler, "Way to go, Rina!"

A stunned look appears on Mrs. Hancock's face and she orders me to retrieve the book. Just then the bell rings and everyone starts to file out of the classroom.

Mrs. Hancock comes over to my side and in a concerned voice says, "I wouldn't have expected that type of behavior from someone like you, Rina, someone who loves reading the way you do."

"It's a stupid book," I mumble, picking it up off the floor and running out of the classroom before she has time to scold me any further.

In my fourth period History class, I can't stop thinking about Mom. I don't understand how she can act so cowardly. Why can't she see how much this is hurting me, hurting little Joey and Carmen? I don't understand why she doesn't kick Dad out for good.

At lunchtime, Juanita, Ankiza and Maya are waiting for me at my locker. They each give me a hug and tell me how happy they are that I'm back in school. On the way over to meet the guys, Maya fills me in on the lastest news at Roosevelt—that Mary Gibson broke up with Sean, who's severely depressed, and that Shane got busted for smoking pot. I don't know how Maya does it, but she knows everyone and everything that goes on at our school. I guess that's 'cause she's so popular, everyone likes her. Me, I'm pretty much invisible. Half the kids here don't even know I exist. But I really don't care. I don't need anyone to like me.

At the football field, Tommy, Tyrone, Rudy and a new guy named Gus are already waiting on the bleachers for us. Tommy scoots over so Ankiza and I can sit next to him. Like always, Maya sits with Tyrone while Juanita joins Rudy and Gus who are one row below Tommy. It turns out that Gus just moved here from Los Angeles and it's his first day of school.

I say hello to everyone except Rudy. He still gives me the creeps. I don't like his attitude and I still hold it against him the way he acted when he found out Tommy was gay. He asked questions like, "Is Tommy going to try and hit on me?"

When Tommy asks me how my classes went, I imitate Mrs. Plumb's Spanish pronunciation and tell him, "¡Estupendo!" Everyone laughs and Rudy turns to me and says, "Hey, Rina, did you hear what happened in Spanish the other day? Jesús Rosales was conjugating a verb on the board and at the end he wrote *Con Safos*. When Mrs. Plumb asked Jesús what that meant, he answered, "It means, with l-o-v-e. *Póngase trucha, Señora* Plumb." Some kids started laughing and old

Mrs. Plumb freaked. She thought Jesús had used a cuss word so she sent him to the office."

Maya repeats loudly, "What an idiot!" and we all break into laughter.

In my afternoon classes, a couple of students ask me why I missed school, and I explain that I had to stay home to help my grandmother who was very ill. It doesn't make me feel very good that I lie, but I know I can't tell the truth. Anyway, it's nobody's business.

After school, I reluctantly get on the school bus. It's packed with noisy students. I end up having to share a seat with a nerdy redhead from my History class whose name I can't even remember. When she asks me how I did on today's quiz, I say, "What's it to you?" Then I dig out my copy of *The Scarlet Letter* from my backpack and start flipping through it, hoping she got the hint. By the time I get to my bus stop, I'm already getting to know Hester Prynne and her messed-up life.

As I step inside the apartment, Abuela turns away from her afternoon telenovela and asks, *"¿Cómo te fue en la escuela, hija?"*

"Okay. Is that *La última pasión?*"

"Yes, *hija*. And tomorrow is the wedding, but Camelia doesn't know that José Andrés hasn't been feeling well. I think he's going to die soon."

"Good," I mumble under my breath, but Abuela doesn't hear me because her attention is focused back on Claudia and José Andrés. I go into the kitchen and help myself to some cookies and a soda. Then I pick up the telephone and dial my home number. After a few rings, I hear Mom's voice say, "Hello." I hesitate for a moment before I finally say, "Mom. It's me, Rina."

"*M'ija*. How are you?" Mom greets me good-naturedly.

"What do you think?" I answer coldly.

"*M'ija*, we all miss you terribly."

"Yeah, I bet you do. Is Creepo home?"

"Rina, don't talk that way about your dad," Mom whispers in a flat, dead voice.

"He's not my real dad and I can talk about him any way I want," I say angrily. "Anyway, I didn't call to talk to you. Put Carmen on the phone."

Mom doesn't say another word to me and I know I've hurt her.

Carmen comes on the line. The first thing she does is ask if I'm coming home soon. I tell her that I can't just yet. She insists on knowing the reason why, but I tell her that it's too complicated to explain. When I ask her if she's being good in school, Carmen answers happily, "Yeah, I was star of the week and I got to take in a bunch of things from home and put them on the bulletin board. I even took a picture of me, you and Joey."

"That's good," I answer, feeling as if I want to cry. I never thought I'd miss Carmen as much as I do. It seems like all I ever did was boss her around or yell at her to stay out of my things.

"How's Joey?" I finally ask.

Carmen says, "He's nothing but a cry-baby. He keeps waking up at night, saying he's afraid of the dark."

"Do you leave a night light on for him?"

"Yeah, but he still wakes up crying."

"Then let him sleep in your bed so he won't be afraid."

Carmen lets out a sigh of frustration. "Yeah, I know. That's what Mom told me to do. But the other night he peed in my bed."

"Can I talk to him now?"

"Yeah, let me go get him," Carmen says.

In the background I hear her calling out for little Joey, and a few seconds later a tiny voice greets me. "Hi, Rina. Are you coming home today?"

"Not yet," I answer sadly. "But I will soon."

"Tomorrow?" Joey asks hopefully.

"No, but I promise I will real soon. Remember the teddy bear I won at the carnival last year?"

"You mean the big purple one?"

"Yeah, that one. You can have it." Little Joey screams with delight. "But you have to take him to bed with you at night 'cause he's very lonely all by himself since I left."

"He'll sleep with me every night," little Joey agrees. Then he says, "Have to go. Power Rangers are on. Bye."

I smile to myself, hoping that now Joey won't be so afraid at night. When I hear Mom's voice come back on the line, I abruptly tell her that I have to go, leaving her sentence hanging in mid-air.

The, as I turn around, Abuela is staring at me with those owl-like eyes of hers. "I don't understand why your mom can't be a good wife," she tells me. "She should quit that awful job and stay home."

I shout angrily, "You don't understand anything, Abuela! Just leave Mom alone!" Then I take off to my bedroom and slam the door behind me.

Twelve

Rina

On Wednesday, Tommy and Ankiza invite me to Foster Freeze at lunchtime. Maya and Juanita don't come with us 'cause they want to spend time alone with Tyrone and Rudy. Me, I'm glad I don't have a boyfriend. As far as I'm concerned, most guys are nothing but pigs.

On the way to Foster Freeze, Tommy tells us about the new CD he bought by some weird guy named El Vez who sings Elvis songs. While Tommy describes some of the songs on the CD, I start to space out. I write a poem in my head. A sad clown poem. No one knows that I like to write poetry. Not even Maya. But I have notebooks filled with poems, even some in Spanish. Lately, it seems like all I care to do is write sad poems.

"Hey, girl, I'm talking to you," Ankiza says, pinching me lightly on the arm.

Tommy snaps his fingers at me, repeating, "Earth calling Rina. Earth calling Rina. Come in, Rina."

"Shut up, Tommy," I tell him, smiling.

Ankiza repeats her question to me. "Do you wanna go to the movies with us on Friday? We're gonna go see the new *Hellraiser* movie. It's playing downtown."

"Forget it," I tell her. "You know I hate scary movies."

"Come on, Rina. It's *Hellraiser 6*." Then he starts to chant out loud, *"Hellraiser, Hellraiser,"* and I punch him playfully in the arm until he finally stops it.

Foster Freeze is packed today, and it takes us a while longer to get our burgers and shakes. We end up sitting outside on one of the small cement tables and I'm really glad I wore my sweatshirt 'cause it's breezy and overcast. I'm about to finish the last bite of my double cheeseburger, when Ankiza pokes me on the arm and says, "Isn't that your dad's car?"

I turn to look on the other side of the street and sure enough, Dad's car is parked in front of a red-brick office building. I recognize his red, green and white Mexican flag bumpersticker. Just then, Dad comes walking up the street with a woman I've never seen before. When they get to his car, Dad opens the door for her. Their shoulders touch for a brief moment and I watch in disgust as Dad kisses her on the lips.

"Don't look, Rina," Tommy advises me sympathetically, but my eyes remain glued to Dad's car as they drive away together.

"Sorry, Rina," Ankiza tells me.

"Nothing to be sorry about," I repeat, feeling as if my face is on fire. "He's nothing to me anyway."

Tommy is suddenly on his feet. "Let's go or we'll be late for Spanish. We wouldn't want to give old Mrs. Plumb a heart attack, would we?" he says smiling.

On the way back to campus, I'm angry inside. All I can think about is Dad and his stupid girlfriend.

✎   ✏   ✐

After school, instead of going to Abuela's, I walk to City Park with Minerva, where we hang out until Charley comes by with Mousey and invites us to go cruising. I still don't know if I really like Charley or his friends, but at least they always have a car.

We cruise around Laguna with the radio full-blast until we get hungry and drive to McDonald's for some burgers. Then Charley and Mousey decide that we should get some beer. We go back to the *barrio* to see if Snowball is home. Snowball is the old wino all the kids bum liquor from. I've never met Snowball, but I've seen him lots of times passed out at the small park where we live. They say he never used to drink until his wife died and his son got killed in Vietnam.

Minerva and I wait in the car while Charley and Mousey go talk to Snowball. A few minutes later, they emerge from his apartment carrying a brown paper bag. In the car, Tim flashes a bottle of vodka at us. "Man, did we score!"

"Put it down, *pendejo* , before someone sees it!" I yell.

"Rina's right, *ese*," Charley agrees as we head for the nearest freeway exit.

At Seaside, we go back to the same isolated beach as the other night. We sit on blankets to listen to music, and Mousey hands each of us a can of beer. By now, the sun is going down and the sky is filled with orange-red streaks of light.

"Check out the waves," Minerva says. "They're bad today."

"*Bien truchas*," Mousey says, downing his beer. Then he takes the bottle of vodka out, takes a drink and passes the bottle around.

I feel a burning sensation in my throat as I take a sip from the vodka. I've never had anything that strong before. The next time Mousey offers me a drink, I refuse it. Minerva calls me a chicken, but I tell her to shut up.

I'm finishing my second beer when I feel Charley place his arm around my waist. I'm about to tell him to knock it off when I realize how good it feels to be wanted and needed by someone, even if it is just Charley.

"Hey, *ese*, we'll be right back," Mousey suddenly informs Charley. Then, grabbing a blanket, he and Minerva take off holding hands.

Charley reaches for the last can of beer and takes a few drinks. Then he hands it to me and I take a long drink. By the time we finish it, I'm really buzzed. Charley puts his arm around me again and he pulls me closer to him. We start to make out and a warm, tingling sensation spreads throughout my body. Then Charley pushes me gently down on the blanket and we lie next to each other making out. When I feel Charley's cold fingers under my sweater caressing my back, I start to get panicky. I know that I should make him stop, but I can't 'cause it feels good. As Charley unsnaps my bra and moves on top of me, I try to push him away, but he is insistent.

"Come on, *esa*, let's do it," Charley whispers.

At last, I manage to shove him as hard as I can and I get up from under him, threatening to walk home if he doesn't take me home right this minute.

Charley lets out a groan and says, "Okay, okay, I'll take you home."

I know that he's had way too much to drink, 'cause his face is red and his speech is slurred.

Just then, Minerva and Mousey reappear. Minerva's hair is all messed up and there are smudges of lipstick on Mousey's pimpled face. Minerva asks if there's any more beer. Charley tells her it's all gone and that it's time to leave.

When I get home, Abuela is waiting for me in the living room. She looks madder than hell. After she scolds me for not coming home right after school, she asks where I've been, and I mumble that I was at a friend's house. Abuela gives me a mean, hard look, and I'm sure that she can tell I've been drinking. But she doesn't mention it. She orders me to bed, and as I head for my room, she mutters that I'm a *malcriada*, spoiled like my mom.

Thirteen

Ms. Martínez

"How's school?" I asked Rina, who nervously twirled the belt loop that hung from her oversized jeans.

"It's good," she said. "I'm pretty much caught up with the work I missed."

"That's great, because you need to keep an eye on your credits now that you're getting close to graduation. Have you thought about going to college?"

"Are you kidding?" Rina answered sarcastically. "My family doesn't have money for that."

"For your information, young lady, there are many grants and scholarships available to help you pay your way through college. Hasn't anyone at Roosevelt talked to you about them, now that you're a junior?"

"No. But that don't matter, 'cause I'm gonna get a job, save some money and get as far away as I can from this stupid town. Maybe go to New York."

"And why would you want to do that?" I asked, hoping Rina would peel away some of those layers and be open with me.

"'Cause I hate this place."

"What is it exactly that you hate?"

Rina paused, shifting her weight from one side to the other and, after a moment of thought, she blurted out, "I can't stand my parents. Especially Dad. He really pisses me off."

I gazed into Rina's troubled eyes as she continued. "All he does is beat up on Mom and run around with other women. The other day I got so embarrassed. I was at Foster Freeze with some friends and we saw him with one of his girlfriends."

Unable to resist, I was suddenly carried back to my own teenage years. The constant shame. The embarrassment I felt every time one of my friends told me they had seen Dad drunk. Like Rina, I had dreamt of running far away.

Tears flooded Rina's big eyes and her lower lip began to quiver. "I hate him so bad," she went on. "All those lies, telling me that Mom was the one that caused all the problems. After he'd hit her, he always said she deserved it, that she was the one to blame. Then he'd take me and Joey and Carmen shopping and buy us presents. He was always making stuff up. I knew he was the one who punctured mom's tires. He even put sand in her gas tank so she couldn't go to work. I used to pray at night that he'd leave and never come back. Only it never worked. Now I hate him more and I hate myself too."

Rina fought hard to hold back the tears. I handed her a Kleenex, saying, "It's all right to cry, Rina."

"I'm sick of crying, Ms. Martínez," Rina said, looking up at me. "Crying don't do no good. Look at Mom. What good did crying do for her? She just got beat on more and more."

"Rina," I began gently. "Your mom needs to get help, but no one can make her do that. She has to want to seek it out herself."

"I told her to leave him, but she doesn't listen."

"It's not as simple as it seems, Rina. It's not just a matter of telling your mom to leave your dad. Your mom needs outside help, a support network. She needs to know there are people that can help her, people she can rely on emotionally and financially. I have something for you," I said, reaching for a bright green pamphlet on my desk. I handed it to Rina. "Next time you see your mom, give this to her. It's information on the Women's Haven, a shelter for battered women. There's a 24-hour hotline your mom can call if and when she decides she wants help."

Rina examined the brochure carefully. After a few minutes, she exclaimed, "Mom's so stupid. She won't even read it. But I guess I can give it to her anyway."

"That's all you can do, Rina. At least your mom will know that there are places she can turn to for help."

Rina nodded, placing the pamphlet inside her backpack. Her beautiful dark face seemed calmer, more at peace.

"Now, how are you getting along at your grandma's?" I asked, as if to change the subject.

Rina frowned. "Okay, I guess. But she got mad at me last night."

"Why is that?"

"I didn't come home right after school. Me and some friends went to the beach."

"Friends from school?"

"Yeah," Rina said, stretching out her long thick legs. "Minerva's a new friend and I've known Charley since I was in junior high."

Rina hesitated. I waited, not wanting to pressure her.

"It was fun at first . . . we sat around, drank some beer and well, everything was cool except for . . ." Rina paused, leaving her sentence hanging in mid-air.

"Except for what?"

Uncomfortable, Rina looked down at her navy blue sandals. "Well, Charley tried to feel me up. We were both kind of high and he wanted me to go all the way with him."

"And how did you react to that?"

"I don't know. It felt good at first, but then when he wanted more, I got mad and pushed him away."

"Rina, do you know how easy it is to get pregnant or catch a disease? I'm sure you've had sex education at school?"

Rina smiled, looking up at me again. "Yeah, I know about condoms and all that stuff. We had it in Health Ed."

"So you know how careful you have to be?"

"Yeah, but hardly anyone's a virgin any more. Everybody's doing it, so the guys expect it. And Health Ed don't help that much."

"Why is that?"

"'Cause all they do is talk at you. Anyway, Ms. Martínez, I don't plan on having sex for a long time."

"And what happens if Charley tries to pressure you again?"

"Don't worry. I'll punch him so hard he won't *ever* try it again."

I smiled. Rina was certainly not the shy, quiet type. "Instead of hitting someone, what would happen if you just said no?"

Rina thought about this for a moment or two and then said, "Yeah, I guess I could try that."

"That's right, Rina. All you have to say is no, loud and clear. And if that doesn't work, try mentioning fatherhood. Ask the guy if he's ready to drop out of school to support a baby."

"Yeah, that'll definitely scare them," Rina agreed. "Most guys want sex, but don't care what happens afterwards to the girl."

"And be careful about drinking, Rina. Alcohol can make you more emotional and susceptible."

"Yeah, I know," Rina stammered. "I really don't like to drink, but Minerva and my friends do, so . . ."

"Is that a good enough reason for drinking? Because everyone else does it?"

"No, I guess not. But drinking feels good. It makes me forget my problems."

"Can you think of any other things that you can do to help you feel better instead of drinking? What are some of the things that interest you? There must be something you enjoy doing?"

Rina's face lit up. "I like to write poems. But I'm not very good at it."

"That's great, Rina. Have you ever tried publishing any of your poetry?"

"No way, Ms. Martínez. Anyway, who would want to read my stuff?"

"I would."

"You would?"

"Yes, I'd love to. Maybe sometime you'll share some of your poems with me?"

"Are you serious, Ms. Martínez?"

"Of course I am."

"I'd love to be a writer someday," Rina said. "But I'm so stupid, I probably wouldn't even make it through college."

It was sad to hear Rina talk that way about herself. All the more reason why Rina needed something or someone, like me, to give her confidence and motivate her to set goals.

"Dreams do come true, Rina. I'm a living example of that. If you believe in yourself and you work hard, you can be anything you want to be."

"Do you really think so, Ms. Martínez?" Rina sighed heavily.

"Think so? Are you kidding? I *know* so!"

Rina's dark eyes widened with hope, and I was suddenly reminded of a line from a poem someone gave me many years ago: "Water the plant and watch it grow." Before me sat a beautiful flower waiting to bloom. All it needed was some watering.

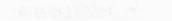

Fourteen

Ms. Martínez

Before I went to bed that evening, my mother called to let me know that Dad would be home on Friday from the hospital. Despite my resistance, the obligation of being the only offspring left in the family always seemed to win out and, by the time I hung up the phone, I found myself promising that I would drive to Delano on Saturday. Frank, of course, was delighted by the idea of spending a weekend with my parents. Over the years, Frank had developed a special relationship with my family. I often teased him that my parents treated him better than they did me. Mom always prepared Frank's favorite Mexican dishes, and Dad enjoyed showing off his *gabacho* son-in-law, as Frank liked to refer to himself, to his *compadres*. At times, I wondered if Frank helped fill the empty space that was left in Mom and Dad's heart after my brother Andy's death.

It was getting close to noon when we pulled into Delano. As we drove through Main Street, I was flooded with memories of growing up in this small farming community that farmworker leaders César Chávez and Dolores Huerta had made famous. As we passed Maldonado's Corner Market, I remembered going there with Andy after school to buy candy. Now all I had left of Andy were these piercing memories. If only he hadn't died so young, things might have been different for my parents. But, then again, who was I trying to kid? Things had been bad long before Andy killed himself.

As Frank parked the car in the driveway, I stared nostalgically at the small two-bedroom house where my parents had lived for the past thirty years. Nothing much had changed. The same wooden frame faded and withered from the hot valley sun. The same sagging fence that surrounded the dried-out front lawn. After all these years, it still looked like a farm laborer's shack. But at least my parents owned it, free and clear, unlike many farmworkers who moved around constantly, never owning their own property. If it hadn't been for the generosity of the farmer in whose orchards Dad had worked until he got too old for field work, this house would never have been theirs to purchase.

Before we got out of the car, Frank turned to me and said, "Now hon, remember, go easy on Mom. She's been through a lot lately."

I nodded reassuringly at him, realizing how much Frank loved and respected my parents.

Mom was standing in front of the stove when I walked into the kitchen. "*Hija*, I didn't even hear your car," she exclaimed, drying her hands on the red checkered apron that hung from her thick waist. Then she reached over and gave me a warm hug. When I asked her for Dad, she explained that he was lying down, adding, "He's still pretty weak, but he'll get up in a while."

Mom's voice sounded drained, and I noticed the dark circles under her tired brown eyes. Her heavy body seemed to pull down on her like a pair of wet rainboots.

Just then, Frank came inside with our luggage. As he reached down to hug Mom, his six-foot-two frame looming above her, he said teasingly, "Are you shrinking, Mom?"

A smile appeared on Mom's wrinkled face. "No, *hijo*, it's you. You're still growing."

"Yeah, I'm growing all right. Right here in the *panza*," Frank replied, patting his stomach.

"Well, at least Sandra's feeding you right, *hijo*," Mom said, smiling again.

I was instantly annoyed by Mom's words. It was a typical attitude in Mexican culture, where women were taught that they were created for the sole purpose of serving their men.

"I made some *caldo*. Are you hungry, *hijo*?" Mom asked Frank, who nodded sheepishly. Frank was *always* hungry! If he wasn't eating a meal, he was snacking. It was always a mystery to me where all those junk-food calories went.

After Mom served Frank, she passed me a bowl of *caldo*, pointing out how thin I was getting.

"I like her that way, Mom," Frank said, his blue eyes twinkling mischievously. "Anyway, too many *panzones* in the kitchen spoil the pot!"

I couldn't help but laugh at Frank. He was such a master at making bilingual jokes. My favorite, of course, was when we toasted and he said, *"Colitas arriba"* for "Bottoms up!"

While we ate, Mom told me about *Don* Mauricio, our next door neighbor since we first moved into the neighborhood. She said that his heart was giving him some problems, but that he stubbornly refused to slow down. Then she talked about her *comadre* Lucía, whose daughter was having a *quinceañera* at the end of the month, describing in detail the lacy, white, wedding-like dress that had been made by a relative in Mexico.

Afterward, we went into the living room to watch television. I was scolding Frank about his obsession with clicking the remote when Dad came out of the bedroom. His face was ashen, and there were more red spots, from broken blood-vessels, on his puffy nose. He greeted us in a low raspy voice which sounded irritated from the tube they had stuck down his throat to stop the bleeding.

I went over to his side and hugged him. "How are you feeling, Dad?"

"Little weak, but better," Dad answered, taking a seat in his brown recliner. Then he turned to Frank and asked him how work was going.

Frank explained he was getting busier now that the income tax deadline was approaching. Then Frank clicked the TV to CNN, knowing how much Dad enjoyed keeping informed on the world news. As soon as the news update ended, Frank invited me to take a nap with him, but I turned him down, hoping that this would be a good time to talk privately with Mom and Dad.

Once Frank was gone, I turned to Dad and asked, "What did the doctor say this time?"

The question was hardly out of my mouth when Mom nonchalantly said, "He's gonna be fine. The doctor said there's no more bleeding."

For a moment, I wanted to tell Mom to shut up. She was always trying to control everyone and everything. I could hear the tension in my voice as I said, "Mom, I know he's okay now. But what about tomorrow? Next week, next month?"

Motionless, Mom didn't respond. Instead, she fixed her gaze on Dad, who acted as if he hadn't heard my question. But I knew that this time I had to get through to him. After all, I hadn't come all the way out here to pretend that everything was fine when it really wasn't.

"Dad," I said as firmly as I could, "isn't it time you got some help before it's too late?"

After a moment or two of dead silence, Dad answered, "I'm going to try the Antabuse pills again."

"Dad, you've tried that before and it hasn't worked. What about Alcoholics Anonymous? There's a chapter here in Delano."

Dad looked up at me, his hazel eyes widening with disgust. "Sandra, how many times have I told you that I don't like to talk in front of strangers? I'm not about to make a fool of myself. Now be quiet and let me watch TV."

Before I could utter a word, Mom snapped at me, "Leave your dad alone, Sandra. Can't you see how weak he is?"

Feeling like a small child who was slapped on the hand, I muttered, "Suit yourself," and left the room angrily.

At dinnertime, a veil of tension separated us. The only cheerful person at the table was Frank. He cracked one silly joke after another while stuffing himself with Mom's homemade *tortillas* and *chile verde.* Every now and then, Dad would smile feebly at Frank's jokes, but most of the time he was quiet and withdrawn. After dinner, we went back into the living room to watch Dad's favorite programs: old re-runs of *Three's Company* and *America's Funniest Home Videos,* and then the network news. When ten o'clock finally rolled around, Dad announced it was time for bed, and I watched sadly as he left the room.

The next morning, as we drove away from my parent's house, I burst into tears. Frank quickly pulled to the side of the road and drew me into his arms. "Don't cry, hon," he whispered soothingly. "You know you can't force your dad to quit drinking. He has to want to do it for himself."

I nodded, remembering how only a few days ago I had given Rina the same advice about her mother. I wondered why it was so hard for me to take my own advice.

Fifteen

Rina

I'm in the back seat of Dad's car with Carmen and Joey, only we're in the middle of the ocean. I can hear little Joey start to cry as I struggle to open the locked door. But it's too late because we're slowly starting to sink deeper and deeper. An alarm begins to go off, ringing and ringing. All of a sudden, it's a telephone ringing—it wakes me up and I realize that I've been having a bad dream. Relieved, I glance at the clock on the nightstand next to me. It's only five o'clock in the morning. The phone won't stop ringing, so I stumble out into the dining room to answer it.

"Hello," I mutter, half-asleep. The place where the living room drapes don't close lets me see that it's still dark outside.

"Rina, can you come for us?" a small, frightened voice whispers.

Suddenly, I'm wide awake. "Carmen, what's wrong? Is Mom okay?"

Carmen's voice breaks, but she manages to answer, "I don't know. She's lying on the floor and she won't move. Rina, please come home." Now Carmen is sobbing loudly.

I can feel my legs get wobbly. It takes all my will power to remain calm. "Carmen, please don't cry. Where's Joey?"

"He—he's right here next to me."

"Is Dad there?"

"No. I think he left," Carmen says in a hushed voice.

My mind is racing like crazy. "Listen carefully, Carmen. You have to be a big girl. Go lock the front door. Then get a blanket and cover Mom. I'm calling 911 and I'll be there as fast as I can. Don't open the door for anyone unless you know who it is."

I hang up quickly and dial 911. I explain what has happened to a calm lady who reassures me that she'll send the police and an ambulance out there immediately. Next, I call Ms. Martínez, 'cause I know she doesn't live too far from Mom's apartment. She offers right away to drive to the apartment to make sure that Carmen and Joey are all right.

By now, Abuela is out of bed. She gets a panicky look on her face when I tell her about Carmen's phone call. Then she orders me to get dressed quickly and go next door to Mr. Montaño's to ask him for a ride.

I catch Mr. Montaño just as he's about to climb into his pickup truck. He agrees to give me a ride and says he goes that way to the hospital where he works as a janitor.

On the way over, Mr. Montaño talks about his grand-daughter, who is one year younger than me, but I'm so nervous that I hardly hear him. When we get to Cabrillo Street, Mr. Montaño drops me off at the corner. I mumble "Thank you," and race down the street to our apartment building. When I get there, I feel a sense of relief when I see Ms. Martínez's old Volkswagen parked next to a Laguna police car.

As soon as I open the door, Carmen and little Joey run up to me. I put my arms around both of them and they cling tightly to me. Ms. Martínez is standing directly behind them, talking with a police officer. She says, "Your Mom's going to be all right, Rina. She was unconscious, but she's going to be fine. The ambulance took her to the hospital."

Unable to speak for fear that I might cry, I nod quietly. The police officer moves toward me and in a kind voice, says, "Your Dad's already been arrested, so you don't have to worry. He won't be causing any more problems tonight." Then he glances at Ms. Martínez and adds, "Dr. Martínez has agreed to take all three of you to your grandmother's house. I'll leave this card with you. It has my name and number in case you need me for anything."

"Thank you," I say, and I reach for the card. Ms. Martínez walks the officer to the door, thanking him one more time before he leaves. Then she comes back and tells me to gather up some of Carmen's and Joey's things so we can take them to Abuela's.

Abuela is at the front door waiting for us when we arrive. She gives little Joey a kiss on the lips and says, *"Pobrecito."* Then she hugs Carmen and orders her to take Joey into the kitchen so they can have a bowl of cereal. Carmen hesitates as if she's waiting for me to say it's okay, and so I tell her to go ahead and do as Abuela says.

As soon as they leave the room, Abuela invites Ms. Martínez to take a seat on the couch. Then she asks her about Mom. Ms. Martínez explains that Mom suffered some bad blows to the head, which knocked her unconscious for a short while, but that she's at the hospital now. Abuela shakes her head sadly, saying, "I don't know why Alma can't do as he says."

Anger starts to rise in me again like a volcano ready to erupt. "How can you defend him after what he did to Mom?" I holler at Abuela, wishing I could shake her so hard that all those stupid thoughts would disappear from her stubborn head.

Ms. Martínez intervenes before I have time to shout any more angry accusations. "It's not Alma's fault, *Doña* Martina. Your daughter is not to blame for anything that has happened to her. I strongly recommend that she get help before it's too late."

Grandma stubbornly refuses to listen, "We don't need anybody's help."

But Ms. Martínez doesn't let Abuela's attitude discourage her. "With all due respect, *Doña* Martina, Alma is the only one who can make that decision. Not you or anyone else. Your daughter needs to know that there are shelters for battered women that can help her if she wants."

Abuela is about to respond when Carmen and Joey come back into the room. Carmen asks me if she and Joey have to go to school today, and Ms. Martínez says that she'll be happy to give us a ride to school on her way to her office. Carmen frowns, but little Joey gets happy at the idea of playing with his friends. Abuela thanks Ms. Martínez and excuses herself, saying that she needs to prepare our lunches.

Ms. Martínez pats me on the hand and says, "Don't worry, Rina. She'll come around. Give her time."

Sixteen

Rina

First we take Carmen and Joey to school, and then Ms. Martínez drives me to Roosevelt High. As I get out of the car, she says that she'll call this evening to set a time for our visit to the hospital. I wave goodbye as she maneuvers her car through the traffic in the busy parking lot. Tommy was right about Ms. Martínez. I don't know what I would have done without her help today.

On my way to my locker, I run into Charley and Mousey, who are standing next to the water fountain browsing through a low-rider magazine. Charley's always bragging about how he's gonna turn his dad's car into a low-rider. When Charley sees me, he whistles at me and I give him a dirty look. I'm uncomfortable around Charley ever since that night at the beach.

Mousey stares at me with his small beady eyes and says, "Hey, Rina, I hear the cops were at your house this morning."

"So what else is new?" I answer sarcastically, hurrying past them before they have time to ask any more questions. I can hear Charley whistle at me again and I feel my blood start to boil. One of these days I'm gonna smash him in the face, tell him he's a real pig. It's no wonder he likes those low-rider magazines.

My morning classes don't go well for me at all. I can't concentrate on anything the teachers are saying because I can't stop thinking about Mom being back in the hospital all beaten up. I'll never understand how she can keep taking this from Dad. Doesn't she have any self-respect? Doesn't she care about me, Carmen and Joey? I hope Dad rots away in jail this time and I hope they never let him out.

In my literature class, my head feels as if it's about to explode from all my angry thoughts, so instead of working on my book report, I decide to write a poem:

> This rage I feel inside
> feeling as if someone died
> wishing I could open up my heart
> feeling as if I'm torn apart.
>
> Help me, I shout to God above.
> I need to find someone to love
> in this life filled with madness
> in this day filled with sadness.

As soon as I finish the last line, I re-read what I've just written. Although it's pretty depressing, it makes me feel better inside. When Mrs. Johnson starts patrolling the aisles, I flip the page in my binder before she has time to notice what I've written. I wouldn't want anyone to read my poetry—especially someone at school.

At lunchtime, Maya, Juanita and Ankiza are waiting for me by my locker. "Snap it up, Rina," Maya tells me. "I'm starved!" I'm not sure how Maya does it, but she eats like a pig and stays skinnier than a bone. Me, I just keep getting fatter and fatter.

As I reach for my sack lunch, Ankiza explains they've decided it's too cold to walk with the guys to Foster Freeze. Here in Laguna everyone's spoiled 'cause it never really gets that cold. In the winter, the temperature rarely gets below sixty degrees. And on foggy days, like today, we usually eat in one of the hallways. Sometimes we like to sit in the enclosed patio area by the main office, but it's generally packed with freshmen.

Today we walk to the Math building and sit in a corner on the floor next to the entrance. There are a group of Gothics camped out at the far end of the hallway, but we don't pay attention to them. They're a bunch of weirdos, always dressed in black as if they're going to a funeral or something.

While Maya, Juanita and Ankiza talk about the senior prom, I don't say much of anything. After a few minutes, Juanita turns to me and says, "I heard your mom's in the hospital again."

Annoyed, I give Juanita the meanest look I can find. "I sure wish people would keep their big mouths shut."

Maya comes to Juanita's rescue. "Hey, Rina! Johnny's just trying to be nice."

With a hurt look on her face, Juanita adds, "Yeah, Rina, I don't mean nothing bad."

"Well, it's nobody's business but mine," I answer angrily.

Ankiza reaches over and pats me on the arm. "Hey, Rina, have you forgotten we're your friends?"

"Yeah, Rina," Maya adds.

They all stare at me. I bet they're wondering how I'll react to their words, I think about whether I should make up another story or tell them the truth. It's hard to trust people anymore, even my own friends.

"Come on, Rina. We're here for you," Juanita says.

I take a deep breath and then I spill my guts. I tell them everything. I even tell them what happened the night I went to live with my grandmother. By the time I'm finished, tears are falling around me. Juanita gives me a Kleenex and Maya puts her arm around me, saying, "Don't worry, Rina. I know your Mom's gonna be fine."

Then Ankiza tells me that she'll ask her dad, who is a doctor at Laguna Hospital, to stop by and check on Mom. All of a sudden, I realize how lucky I am to have friends like Maya, Juanita and Ankiza. I think about *The Scarlet Letter*. Maybe if Hester Prynne had had friends like mine, instead of being all alone, her life wouldn't have been so messed up.

When I get home, little Joey is happily watching *Storm Troopers* while Carmen sits next to Abuela reading a book. Abuela tells me that *Tío* Victor insisted on picking the kids up after school. Carmen looks up from her book to ask if she can go with me and Ms. Martínez to the hospital tonight, but I tell her no. Before she starts to bug me, I head for the kitchen to eat. Today Abuela has made fried chicken. Abuela likes to cook dinner early, so she won't be disturbed while her soap operas are on.

I'm almost finished eating when the phone rings. A minute later Carmen says that Ms. Martínez will come by for me at six-thirty. Carmen asks again if she can go with me to the hospital, but I carefully explain that someone needs to stay with Joey so he won't get lonely.

When Carmen gets a look on her face like she's about to cry, I quickly ask, "Wanna read me a story?" Carmen loves to read out loud to anyone who will listen to her. I don't usually let her, 'cause her voice gets on my nerves, but tonight is different.

Carmen brightens up like a Christmas tree. "Yes!" she exclaims. Then she races out of the room, returning a moment later with a brightly colored book in her hand. "I checked this book out today," she says happily. "It's about a boy named Miguel and his dog, Barkley, who speaks Spanish."

"Let's go read it in my room before Joey's program is over," I tell Carmen, relieved that my plan to cheer her up has worked.

Seventeen

Rina

Ms. Martínez comes by for me at exactly six-thirty. On the way to General Hospital, I tell her that I finally told my friends what happened to Mom—about how Dad beats on her. Ms. Martínez asks me how it felt to tell the truth. I tell her that it helped me to find out what good friends I really have—friends who care about me.

At the hospital, we take the elevator to the third floor. When we get to Mom's room, Ms. Martínez tries to talk me into going in first without her, but I insist that she come inside with me. I'm still pretty shaky after what happened to Mom the other night.

Mom smiles as soon as she sees me. "Rina, *hija*," she says in a faint voice. I've never seen Mom look so bad. There is a small bandage covering her right eyebrow and her hair looks as if she hasn't combed it in weeks.

"Hi, Mom," I say nervously. "Ms. Martínez brought me to see you."

Mom thanks Ms. Martínez and then asks me about Joey and Carmen.

"They're fine. They're with Abuela," I answer.

Mom is quiet for a few moments. Then, with a look of sadness on her bruised face, she tells me, "This time I'm putting a restraining order on your dad."

"Where have I heard that before?" I ask her sarcastically.

"Listen to me, *hija*," Mom replies, pulling herself up against the pillows. "I mean it this time. I never thought your dad would go as far as he did. He almost hurt Joey and Carmen when they wouldn't do what he said. I had to get in his way. I told him he'd have to kill me first, but he wasn't going to hurt my kids."

"I don't believe anything you say. Dad'll get out, beg you to forgive him like he always does, and you'll take him back."

"No, Rina," Mom answers firmly. "Not no more. You have to believe me."

There are tears in Mom's eyes, and for a moment or two I want to believe her, but I know that I can't. I won't let her lie to me any more. I won't let her hurt me again.

Ms. Martínez moves closer to the bed. I think she senses the tension that is mounting inside of me. "Mrs. Morales," she says. "I brought this for you." She hands Mom a green pamphlet, explaining, "It's information about a shelter for battered woman here in Laguna. It's called the Women's Haven. It's an excellent place where many women like you go for help. They can give you a place to stay. They also have counselors and social workers."

Mom carefully examines the pamphlet in her hand before placing it on the nightstand next to her bed.

"It won't do no good, Ms. Martínez," I protest angrily. "She won't read it."

Ms. Martínez ignores my rude remarks and gives Mom a hopeful look, saying, "Everyone has to start somewhere, Rina."

"Thank you, *Doctora* Martínez," Mom says. "I promise I'll read it tomorrow."

"Yeah, right," I mutter to myself. After all, I don't care what Ms. Martínez thinks. In my opinion, Mom's nothing but a no-good liar.

A few days later, we're watching *La última pasión* with Abuela, when Mom comes walking through the front door. Little Joey screams with joy as Mom scoops him up in her arms and carries him to the couch. Then Mom lets go of him so she can hug Carmen, who is waiting patiently at her side. Startled by Mom's unexpected arrival, I simply stare at her. She says hello to me. When Abuela asks how she's feeling, Mom says she's much better, adding, "I came for the kids. We're going to stay at the women's shelter."

Little Joey interrupts to ask, "Is *Papi* coming too?"

Carmen gets a sad look on her face when Mom explains to little Joey that Dad can't live with us anymore. When little Joey looks like he's about to cry, Mom tells Carmen to take him into the bedroom to play while she talks to me and Abuela.

In a stern voice, Abuela begins, "Alma, why don't you go back home? You don't have no business going to one of those places."

The worry lines on Mom's high forehead deepen as she answers Abuela in Spanish, "No. I can't go home yet. I need some help and the women's shelter will help me and the kids."

"What will people say?" Abuela exclaims in Spanish, shaking her head disgustedly.

Still speechless, I listen to Mom defend herself. "I don't care what anyone says. All I care about is me and the kids. I'm not going to let José hurt us any more."

Angered by Mom's defiant stance, Abuela mutters something in Spanish that I don't understand and leaves the room. I sit there motionless. I've never heard Mom talk to Abuela like this before.

"Rina, I'd like for you to come with us," Mom says softly. "The Women's Haven is a real nice place. They already have a room for us and they told me they have kids your age there too."

There's a struggle going on inside of me. I want to believe that Mom is serious, but I'm afraid to trust her again. "Why even bother going there?" I blurt out. "Dad's just gonna get out and you'll go back with him right away."

Mom shakes her head sadly. "I'm sorry if I've hurt you, Rina, but this time I'm never taking him back. I know I was wrong to take him back, especially this last time when he hit you. But you've gotta believe me. That's why we're going to the Women's Haven. Won't you please come with us, *hija*?"

I'm unable to move or even speak from the tornado of fear that has suddenly sucked me into its path. "I can't. I just can't," I finally say, biting down hard on my lower lip to keep myself from crying.

"*Hija*," Mom pleads, "don't you believe I can change?"

Just then, Carmen and little Joey come back into the room. Joey has already put on his shoes and coat. "Aren't you coming too, Rina?" he asks.

I smile feebly, reaching down to tighten the shoelace on Joey's left shoe. "Maybe she'll come later, *hijo*," Mom tells him reassuringly.

"Will you, Rina?" Carmen asks earnestly.

There is a long moment of silence before I'm finally able to answer Carmen's question. "Maybe later," I whisper, and a glimmer of hope appears on Mom's weary face.

Eighteen

Ms. Martínez

It was almost time for my appointment with Rina. I was hoping that by now she'd softened up her attitude toward her mother and had decided to join her at the Women's Haven. But I had to be realistic. Rina needed time to work out her anger and resentment. After all, she was bruised and battered herself from living a childhood filled with crises, emotional bruises, and fears for her mother's life.

The sudden ringing of the telephone forced me back to the moment at hand. A familiar voice greeted me. "Sandra, I almost didn't recognize you. You sound so businesslike."

An alarm went off inside of me and I leaned back into my chair. Mom never called me at the office unless it was an emergency. "Mom, is anything wrong?" I asked.

Mom sighed heavily and said, "I hated to call you, Sandra. But I didn't know what else to do."

"It's Dad, isn't it?"

"Yes, Sandra. I caught him drinking again. He was hiding beer in the bedroom and sneaking drinks when I wasn't around."

Silence filtered into the room. I fixed my gaze on the barren tree outside my window. Helpless and alone, it seemed to summon me with its skinny arms.

"I don't know what to do, *hija*," Mom continued, releasing a few sobs. "Your Dad's killing himself. He doesn't give a damn about me or anybody."

"Mom, I tried to tell you that when I was there, but you and Dad refused to listen," I said, trying hard to keep my voice under control.

"Well, I just can't take it anymore. I feel like I'm gonna have a nervous breakdown. I told him I'm gonna leave him if he doesn't quit drinking."

"Mom, please try to understand. No one can make Dad quit drinking except himself. If Dad won't go to AA meetings, how about you Mom? There are Al-Anon meetings for the spouses and children of alcoholics."

"*¡Estás loca, Sandra!* I couldn't do that."

"Why not, Mom? I know it would help. I have clients who attend Al-Anon meetings all the time. It helps them to understand alcoholism as a disease and how it affects each member of the family. Won't you at least think about it, Mom?"

"I don't know, *hija*."

"Remember my high school friend, Sarah Johnson? The one you used to like so much? Well, she's the director of an Al-Anon and an Alateen program in Delano. I know she'd be glad to take you with her to a meeting."

Mom hesitated, but before she had time to refuse my offer to help, I added, "It's all settled, Mom. I'll call Sarah this evening."

After I hung up with Mom, I hurried out to the kitchen for a cup of herbal tea to calm my nerves. When I came back, Rina was sitting on the couch waiting for me.

"Hi, Ms. Martínez," she greeted me cheerfully as I sat down at my desk.

"Hello, Rina. I'm glad you made it. I've been sitting here thinking about you."

"You have?" Rina exclaimed.

"Of course. How are things between you and your mom?"

Rina sighed. "Well, I guess you already know that Mom took Joey and Carmen with her to live at that women's shelter you told her about."

"Yes. Your mom and I talked about it before she left the hospital. How do you feel about her decision to stay at the Women's Haven?"

Rina slumped down on the couch, stretching out her long legs in front of her. "I don't know. I guess it's good. And Mom said she finally put a restraining order on Dad. That's hard to believe. But she keeps begging me to go stay with her. Abuela says it's a stupid idea."

"Have you ever been to a women's shelter, Rina?"

"Nope."

"The Women's Haven provides financial and emotional support for battered women so they can get away from their abuser and learn to regain control of their lives. Your mom will meet other women who are going through the same experiences. It's a very good program."

Rina remained quiet for a few minutes. Then she leaned forward and said, "Ms. Martínez, do you think I should go check it out?"

"Yes, Rina, I do. It might help you to understand what your mother has been going through all these years."

I waited patiently while Rina brushed away the tears that were sliding down her face. If Rina only knew how miserable I myself felt after Mom's unexpected phone call. At last, Rina spoke. "I'll think about it, Ms. Martínez."

"Good girl," I said, reaching over and patting her on the hand.

Later that evening, I picked up the phone and called my friend Sarah Johnson. After finishing her degree in social work, Sarah had moved back to Delano, where she now headed up several programs. Sarah and I had lost touch with each other after high school, but several years ago we ran into each other at a weekend seminar in Laguna. From that day on, we made it a point to keep up with each other, even if it was only three times a year.

I spent the first few minutes talking to Sarah about my busy work schedule and how Frank and I were becoming experts on microwaved dinners. When I asked Sarah about her family, she told me her two teenage sons were driving her and her husband crazy. Raging hormones, I teased her, reminding her that we had once been that way. Sarah laughed, telling me that she would send her sons to me so I could straighten them out. At last, I explained to Sarah the reason for my phone call.

"Of course, I'll help, Sandy. I'll call your mother tonight. The first time is always the hardest."

I thanked Sarah several times, and hung up the phone with a sense of relief and satisfaction. I knew that if anyone could convince Mom to attend an Al-Anon meeting, it was Sarah. After all, Mom had always preferred Sarah over any of my girlfriends.

Nineteen

Rina

On Monday, Tommy offers to give me, Maya and Ankiza a ride home in his dad's car. We're grateful not to have to take the bus because it's always crowded with dorky-looking guys. Now I remember how Maya and Ankiza always envied the fact that Juanita and I could walk home after school instead of riding the stupid bus.

When we pull up to Maya's house, she begs me and Tommy to go in with her and Ankiza, telling us that we'll have the house all to ourselves until six o'clock. Maya's parents were divorced last year, and now she lives in this big house with her mom, who is a professor at Laguna University. Maya is persistent, but I tell her I can't, and Tommy explains that he promised his dad he'd get the car home right after school. Disappointed, Maya sticks her tongue out at us as while Ankiza happily waves goodbye.

As we drive away, Tommy shakes his head, saying, "That Maya sure is a pain. It's a wonder Tyrone puts up with her. It's a wonder anyone puts up with her."

"Yeah, but she's down," I say even though I know exactly what he means. At times, Maya does act like a selfish spoiled brat and she can't even see it.

Tommy asks, "Are you still hanging out with Minerva?"

I hesitate for a few seconds before getting up my nerve to answer. "Yeah, we talk on the phone, but now that I'm living at Abuela's, I don't see much of her. Why do you ask?"

"Cause she's bad news, that's why," Tommy says, giving me a disapproving look.

"Don't worry, I can take care of myself."

"Yeah, sure," Tommy says as he drives toward the south side of Laguna. "Like you did that night at the beach?"

"Shut up," I say, turning up the radio. I start to sing along with the song that's playing, but Tommy doesn't let that bother him.

"Have you seen your Mom since she got out of the hospital?"

"Yeah, she came for Carmen and little Joey the other night. They're staying at the shelter that Ms. Martínez told her about—the Women's Haven."

"Oh, yeah?" Tommy says, surprised. "I heard about that place. It's supposed to be pretty nice."

"Mom keeps begging me to go visit her, but I don't want to."

"Why not?"

"I don't know," I shrug. "It seems stupid to go to a place like that."

Tommy is quiet while he turns onto the busy street where Abuela lives. After a few moments, he glances at me and says, "There's nothing stupid about going to the Women's Haven. Maybe they can help your mom."

"Yeah, that's what Ms. Martínez thinks, too. She said they have support groups or something like that. Mom wants me to go with her to one of them, but I think it's stupid talking in front of a bunch of strangers."

"It's not stupid to do that, Rina."

"How would you know?" I ask indignantly.

"Didn't Maya tell you I go to a support group myself?"

I'm feeling like real stupid now. If there's anyone's feelings I don't want to hurt, it's Tommy's. "I'm sorry, I didn't mean it like it sounds," I quickly apologize.

"Don't sweat it. Not too many people know it," Tommy explains as he parks the car in front of Abuela's duplex.

"What's it like at those support groups? Aren't you embarrassed?"

Tommy turns to look at me with his penetrating green eyes. "At first I was embarrassed, but after a while I started to realize that all these other people were having the same experiences as me and it made me feel better. I began to feel like I wasn't all alone. The group even helps me understand where Dad's coming from, why he can't accept me."

I don't say another word for fear that I might start to cry. If anyone knows what it's like to feel helpless and alone, it's Tommy. At last, I'm able to speak. "Thanks, Tommy," I say, opening the car door. "I'll think about what you said."

The sad look on Tommy's face disappears and he smiles at me, saying, "Move it, *loca*. Dad'll kill me if I'm late with the car."

Twenty

Rina

In the week that follows, I can't stop thinking about what Tommy and Ms. Martínez said. Maybe they're right. Maybe I should go check out the Women's Haven. When I finally do make up my mind to go there, I tell Abuela and I'm shocked that she doesn't try to talk me out of it. Instead, she bakes some cookies to take to Carmen and Joey.

On Saturday morning, I take the city bus downtown. It drops me off a few blocks from the two-story peach colored house that they made into the Women's Haven. At the front door, I carefully follow the instructions on the wall and press the small white buzzer. A few seconds later, the door opens and a tall middle-aged woman with warm eyes invites me inside. Her name is Karla, and she is the weekend counselor and "group facilitator," she tells me. I'm about to give her Mom's name when little Joey comes bolting down the hallway, shouting, "Mom, Mom, Rina's here!"

Embarrassed, I grab onto little Joey's hand, ordering him to settle down. But Karla reassures me that it's all right, that they're used to kids here. Just then, Mom appears in the brightly lit hallway. Her face breaks into a big smile as soon as she sees me. *"M'ija*, I'm so glad you came," Mom says.

All the while, little Joey is tugging at my sleeve. "Rina, come see the playroom," he pleads. Karla smiles at little Joey and, before she goes back into her office, she tells Mom to give me a complete tour of the house.

With little Joey leading the way, we go down the hallway and turn left into a large room filled with all kinds of toys. At one end of the room, there are three children playing on the floor who appear to be about little Joey's age. "That's my friend, April," little Joey exclaims, pointing to a freckle-faced girl who is building something with red and black Legos. As soon as April sees Joey, she asks him to come play with her. Mom tells Joey to go ahead, but he hesitates, looking up at me. When I promise to come by for him after I've finished touring the house, Joey happily races across the room to join April.

First, we visit the rooms on the main floor. Directly across from the playroom is a good-sized room, which Mom refers to as the TV room. Mom introduces me right away to two women seated on one of the two couches, reading magazines. One of them is around Mom's age, but the other one only looks a few years older than me. Mom points to the TV and tells me that no one is allowed to turn it on between 9 a.m. and 3 p.m. She explains that everyone who lives here is assigned daily house chores and that there is a strict 9 p.m. bedtime rule for all the kids. When I ask how many people live at the shelter, Mom says that they only have room for seven women at a time.

Next, we go into a small kitchen which is off to the back of the TV room. It is fairly modern, with a brand-new yellow refrigerator and a matching stove. I notice two microwave ovens, one on each end of the kitchen counter. There is a large kitchen table, which seems to take up most of the space in the room. Mom explains that each family is responsible for their own meals as well as for cleaning up after themselves. She points to the grocery list posted on the refrigerator door, saying that each family gets to put things on the list, which are then purchased by the shelter once a week.

From there, we head to the back of the main floor, where there are four bedrooms and two bathrooms. Mom's bedroom is the one on the far right. She opens the door and shows me the double bed where she sleeps. Across from her, there is a bunk bed. Although the room is painted a bright rose color, it still seems like a sad place to me. I guess I really miss our old apartment.

"Joey loves the bunk beds," Mom says. "But Carmen hates sleeping on the top. She thinks she's gonna roll off."

Before we go upstairs, Mom takes me to the back porch and outside to the enclosed yard where there are several swing sets as well as a small playhouse. Two women are talking to each other while they push their kids on the swings.

"Carmen spends most of her time out here," Mom says.

I catch a glimpse of two girls inside the playhouse. One of them looks like Carmen, but we leave before I can catch her eye.

Upstairs, Mom quickly points out three more bedrooms. Then she takes me downstairs to the basement. In the basement, there are several offices which are used by the counselors. When we come to the end of the hall, Mom pauses before opening the door. *"M'ija,* this is where the group meetings are held," she says timidly.

"What are they?" I ask nonchalantly, taking in the two small couches and the metal folding chairs that fill up the large room. My eyes stop to rest on the colorful painting on the wall. It's a country scene with an old red farmhouse, green rolling hills in the background and the bluest sky I've ever seen. I find myself wishing I lived there, surrounded by all that peacefulness.

"Well," Mom starts to explain, "it's different every day of the week. Sometimes we have what they call a 'rap group.' It's for everyone who lives here, and we get to talk about anything we want. Then there's a family hour with the kids, where we talk about problems that come up or things that bother us. Today, we're having a meeting with Karla for anyone who wants to come. They don't have to be living here."

There is a slight pause and then Mom asks, "Rina, will you stay for the group meeting? It starts right after lunch, and Karla already told me it would be all right if you came."

Unable to resist Mom's pleading eyes, I agree, and she smiles happily, reaching over to give me a giant hug.

Twenty-One

Rina

Carmen is even more excited than little Joey to see me at the Women's Haven. While she wolfs down a hot dog, she tells me all about the new friends she's made and the club they've formed. When Joey asks if he can visit their club, Carmen exclaims, "No way, Joey! No boys are allowed inside our clubhouse." Little Joey starts to pout, but he cheers up as soon as I tell him that someday he'll be old enough to form his own club.

When we're finished eating, Carmen and little Joey hurry off with their friends while Mom and I head downstairs for the meeting. We take a seat next to a tall brunette, whose name is Marie. While Mom talks with Marie, I stare at the women who are coming into the room. It surprises me to see a few pregnant women in the group. By the time Karla arrives, there are about twelve women of various ages sitting around me.

Karla opens the meeting by reminding everyone that anything that is said among us does not leave the room.

Then she introduces me as Alma's daughter. I'm so nervous that all I manage to do is whisper "Hi."

The next thing Karla does is ask Marie how things have been going for her lately.

Marie leans forward and says, "I finally realize I'm not ugly and that nothing is wrong with me. For the longest time, my abuser made me think something was wrong with me. But now I know it's him and all the anger he was raised with. I've learned so much from being here. My abuser always said I was the problem. He made me feel like I always did everything wrong. I dressed wrong. I even vacuumed wrong. He told me everything was wrong about me and I believed it."

A broad-shouldered woman sitting next to Marie, joins in. "I know exactly what you mean. My abuser made me feel degraded. Now I know I don't have to be perfect or the one who takes care of everyone else. What I wonder is, if they're so abusive, how is it that they hid it so well from us in the beginning?"

"Yeah, I know that feeling," a round, gray-haired lady interjects. "My old man said I made him the way he is. But I'm stronger now. I realize he's the one with the problems. Not me."

Karla waits until there is a slight pause in the conversation, then she turns to the pretty lady sitting next to her and asks, "Joanne, have you had any recent contact with your abuser?"

Joanne, who looks like she's the youngest in the group, responds, "Only by phone. I keep asking my son if he wants to see his daddy and he tells me, 'No, Daddy's bad. He hurts Mommy.'"

The tired-looking woman on the other side of Joanne, speaks up. "My two kids are so hurt now, the only way they can show it is by getting angry. But the other night, I finally got my thirteen-year-old to cry. I held her in my arms and we both cried together."

Karla peers into the woman's sunken eyes and asks, "And what about you, Connie? Do you cry more now?"

Connie sighs heavily. After a moment she answers, "Yes, I do. And I'm finding out that it's okay to cry. But I don't know if I'll ever be able to forgive myself for what my abuser made me do that time when Mom was dying of cancer. He wouldn't let me go stay with her." Connie's voice breaks and tears start to run down her thin cheeks.

Joanne reaches over and pats her on the hand. "Don't beat yourself up for that, honey," she says. "We all do the best we can."

In a comforting voice, Karla compliments Connie on the tremendous growth she's experienced since she left her abusive relationship. A thin blonde woman starts talking about how the best thing she ever did was leave her abuser and come to the Women's Haven. "Yeah, I was ready to kill myself, but everything's better now. I have myself. I have my children and I have God. That's all I need."

Karla nods her head, saying, "Did it help to come here and work on your self-esteem?"

The blonde lady nods her head. "Yes. I learned to do affirmations. And to admit I needed help."

Karla glances around the room at the group of women and repeats firmly, "Yes. It's very important to get support from each other and from our support groups. Your individual families can try to help you, tell you what you should do, but you need to know where else you can get help."

All of the women nod in agreement with what Karla has just said, including Mom. Then, Karla turns to one of the pregnant girls on the couch and asks, "How are you feeling, Melissa?"

Melissa half-smiles. "Oh, I'm feeling weak, trying to get my strength back. The doctor said I'm having twins. And I went to see a lawyer today and he's going to get the paperwork for the divorce started." Melissa bows her head slightly, but not before I notice the tears in her eyes.

"Getting a divorce is not easy," Karla comforts her. "It hurts a lot."

A big, stern-faced lady, who reminds me of a truck driver, blurts out sarcastically, "Tell me about it! It's been hell getting a divorce from my abuser."

The truck-driver lady's remark brings on a discussion about how the police and the law seem to protect the men more than the battered women. Karla listens patiently while the women air their frustrations. When they finally quiet down, she turns to the young Latina sitting next to the truck-driver lady and says, "Won't you introduce yourself to the group?"

In a soft, shy voice, the dark-skinned Latina tells Karla that her name is Alicia.

Karla welcomes her to the group, saying, "I know this is your first time here. Do you feel like talking?"

Alicia hesitates for a very long minute until she at last has the courage to speak. "I'm going to court to get a restraining order this week, and I'm so scared. I don't know what he'll do." I recognize the look of fear on Alicia's face while my mind flashes back to the night I left home.

Karla is about to speak when a redhead, whose name is Myrna, tells Alicia that she knows it's a hard thing to do because she had to do the same thing a few weeks ago. Then she asks Alicia if she knows the judge's name. Alicia tells her his name is Judge Madison, and Myrna says, "That one's not so bad."

Connie turns to Alicia and says, "Don't be afraid, hon. If we can do it, you can do it too."

I'm surprised when Mom, who has been silent throughout the entire session, finally speaks. "I'm real scared too. But I realize it's better to be alone than being afraid day in and day out for your life and your kids' lives."

Mom reaches out for my hand and for the first time I realize that she's not a coward, that she's brave, like all the women in this room. Guilt starts to gnaw at me as I remember all the times I yelled at Mom and told her she was a stupid fool for letting Dad beat on her.

Gina, a tall black woman, says, "I learned something real important too. Now I know what signs to look for. I started to date this man and he got abusive, so I dropped him right away."

Karla tells Gina, "Good for you. It's extremely important to recognize all the signs of an abuser." Then she looks at her watch and announces, "Well, it looks like we're out of time. Is there any final comment anyone would like to make before we all leave?"

The truck-driver lady says, "All I know is, I'm never gonna get in this situation again."

In a loud voice, Gina says, "Amen."

Laughter breaks out, and the tension in the room begins to disappear.

Twenty-Two

Ms. Martínez

"You're looking very pretty today," I complimented Rina. She was wearing a bright red knit top with a pair of polyester pants which reminded me of the bell-bottomed pants worn in the '70s.

"Thanks, Ms. Martínez," Rina smiled, pressing her lips together.

"How have you been doing?"

A puzzled look appeared on Rina's face. "Okay, I guess. I went to visit Mom at the shelter."

"That's great. I'll bet your mother was very happy to see you."

"Yeah, she was. She showed me the whole place. She even took me to one of her group meetings."

"And what did you think of it?" I asked, amazed that Rina had actually attended a support meeting.

Rina paused, shifting her weight from one side to the other. "To tell you the truth, Ms. Martínez, I really didn't want to go—all those women like Mom who get beat on all the time. But now I'm really glad I went."

"And why is that?"

Rina hesitated for a moment while she searched for the right words. "Well, I guess listening to all those women made me see that Mom's not the one to blame. You know, I've been so mad, blaming Mom all the time. Now I think I understand a little better what she's been going through."

"That's great, Rina."

"Some of the women even talked about how their kids feel angry and scared. It made me think of me."

"And how is that?"

"I've been so pissed off at Mom, at everyone. I guess I've been just as scared as Mom all these years."

I nodded, pleased that Rina was recognizing her mother's feelings as well as her own.

"Mom's moving back to the apartment next week. She wants me to come home with her, Carmen and Joey."

"Have you reached a decision yet?" I asked gently.

Rina frowned. "I don't know, Ms. Martínez. I want to go back home, but I'm so afraid."

"Afraid of what?"

"I'm still so afraid she'll let Dad come back again. I know I can't go through that anymore and I don't want Joey and Carmen to either."

I knew how Rina felt, thinking back to all the years I had stayed away from my parents' home, unable to cope with Dad's alcoholism and Mom's denial that he had a problem.

"But Mom swears she'll never let him back."

"And how do you feel about trusting her on that?"

"I want to, but I'm scared," Rina replied, tears stinging her big dark eyes.

"I know it's difficult, Rina. But sometimes we need to give the people we love another chance."

"Yeah, maybe," Rina whispered at last, a distant look on her beautiful face.

✎ ✐ ✐

After Rina left, I dialed my mother's number in Delano. It rang a few times before Mom finally picked it up.

"Sandy, I was just about to call you," she said, sounding happy.

I don't know how Mom did it, but she always sensed when I needed to talk with her. "How's Dad?"

"Está bien. He hasn't been drinking for a few days now."

"That's good," I said, feeling the weight begin to lift from my shoulders.

"Sandra, the reason I was going to call you was to let you know that I went to one of those meetings the other night."

"You did?"

"Yes. Your friend Sarah called and she talked me into going to a meeting with her. She even came to pick me up."

I smiled to myself, wondering what in the world I'd have done all these years without good friends like Sarah Johnson. "And how did you like the meeting?"

"Bueno, hija. At first I was embarrassed, but then as I sat and listened to all these men and women talk about what it was like being married to an alcoholic, well, I felt better. I realized that many people go through the same thing I do with your dad."

"That's why I wanted you to go, Mom. So that you could see you're not alone."

"Qué bueno, hija. And Sarah says she's taking me again next week. She's a nice girl."

"Yes, Sarah really cares about people."

"She's a lot like you, *hija.*"

It took me a few seconds before I was able to register what I had just heard. My mom, who was always criticizing me, was giving me a compliment! Absolutely unbelievable! I thanked Mom, telling her that Dad might come around once he saw she was attending the meetings.

We chatted for a few more minutes about Dad's health and my next visit to Delano. It wouldn't be until after Frank's April tax deadline at work. By the time we said goodbye, I felt a sense of satisfaction. First Rina and now Mom.

Twenty-Three

Rina

The TV is blaring with the latest episode of *La última pasión* while I try to do my math homework.

"*Ay, m'ija*, José Andrés is going to *kiss* her," Abuela sighs loudly as the handsome leading man pulls Camelia into his arms and showers her with flowery words of his undying love.

I laugh sarcastically. If only life were really that perfect. If only my real dad had been like José Andrés and loved Mom instead of beating on her, maybe things would have been different for all of us.

My fantasy is suddenly interrupted when Joey comes running through the front door. Behind him are Mom and Carmen.

"Guess what, Rina?" little Joey says, giving me a hug. "We're back home."

"Oh, yeah, I can see that!" I tease him as he goes over to hug Abuela who has finally lowered the volume on the TV.

Mom takes a seat on the couch next to her mother and Carmen comes up to me and says, "We came to get you, Rina."

Mom opens her mouth to say something when Abuela interrupts her, asking if it's true that she's moved back to the apartment. Looking as if she's struggling to remain calm, Mom explains that last night was their first night back home. Then Abuela asks in Spanish if José is moving back as well. Mom forcefully explains that she will never allow Dad to come home again. Abuela gets an angry look on her dark wrinkled face. She interrogates Mom about how she plans on supporting three kids on her own. Mom doesn't let Abuela get to her. In a calm, assertive tone, she answers, "I'm going to do it. That's all there is to it."

For once, Abuela doesn't argue. Instead, she tells Mom she's going to make some coffee and disappears into the kitchen.

Mom gets sad, but seems to cheer up when I tell her, "Don't worry, Mom. Abuela will get over it."

"Come on, Rina," Carmen says grabbing my hand. "I'll help you pack."

"Me too," Joey says.

I hesitate, unsure of what I should do next.

"Rina," Mom tells me, reassuringly. "I need you with me. And Joey and Carmen need you too. We all need you."

Tears sting my eyes as I let Carmen and little Joey lead me into the bedroom to get my things.

Back at the apartment, the first thing I do is go into my bedroom, where I lie down on my bed and let my eyes wander around the room. Then I stare at all my posters on the wall, letting my eyes rest on the little wooden jewelry box, on top of my dresser, that Maya gave me for Christmas last year. It's funny, but I've never missed any of my things until now. I guess it's good to be back home.

The next morning at school, Maya insists we all go to Foster Freeze at lunchtime to celebrate my homecoming. Maya is always looking for an excuse to celebrate, but this time I don't mind. Going home *is* something to celebrate.

At Foster Freeze, I talk about my visit to the Women's Haven and how it turned out to be okay. Maya agrees with me, saying how her Mom's been there to speak and it's a great place for women to get help.

When Juanita asks if I miss Dad, I tell her, "Are you kidding? I hate his guts." Tyrone laughs, and Tommy adds, "I know what you mean. I can't stand being around my dad. As soon as I graduate, I'm outta there."

Rudy, who has been pigging out on everybody's french fries, says, "Yeah, me too. I'm going as far away from this town as I can."

Then Maya announces cheerfully, "I've got a great idea! As soon as Dad gets me my car, we can all take off to New York!"

Ankiza pokes Maya in the ribs, calling her a *chica loca*, and Juanita teases her about her bad Spanish pronunciation.

This gets Rudy started on old Mrs. Plumb, the Spanish teacher, and how she wore her sexy silk blouse today.

Tyrone turns to Rudy and tells him, "I think she's got the hots for you. Why don't you ask her out on a date?" We all start laughing and teasing Rudy about Mrs. Plumb.

✎ ✏ ✐

That afternoon, while the science teacher lectures on molecules, I pull out my notebook and write a new poem:

> *Feeling like a butterfly*
> *wings spread wide*
> *don't need to hide.*
> *Feeling like a rainbow*
> *shining so bright*
> *like the morning light.*
> *Feeling like an eagle*
> *soaring so high*
> *no more wondering why.*
> *Feeling.*
> *Breathing.*
> *Being.*
> *Living*
> *Who I am.*

Twenty-Four

Ms. Martínez

"Thanks for cleaning up, hon," Frank told me as I snuggled up on the couch next to him.

"That's the least I can do since you cooked dinner," I replied, staring at Frank, who was engrossed in the mail-order catalog that had just arrived. What in the world was he doing, I thought to myself. If anyone disliked shopping, it was Frank.

"You know, Sandy, your dad's birthday is coming up in a few days. Think he might like this?"

I glanced at the page in the catalog where Frank was pointing to a set of luggage. Puzzled, I turned to him and said, "You want to get Dad a piece of luggage? He never travels."

All of a sudden, Frank was on his feet wiggling his tall lanky body in his best James Brown impression and singing, "Ain't no drag, Papa's got a brand-new bag."

"*¡Ay, Frank, estás bien loco!*" I laughed, tossing the catalog at him.

Just then, the telephone rang, and I hurried back out to the kitchen. I was surprised to hear Rina's voice greet me cheerfully on the other end of the line.

"Hi, Ms. Martínez, hope I'm not interrupting your dinner."

"Not at all, Rina. I'm so happy to hear from you. It's been over a week since we last talked. Your grandma told me you had moved back home."

"Yeah, I'm back at the apartment."

"And how is it going?"

"Everything's real good," Rina answered, pausing for a moment before she went on. "Dad showed up here the other night begging Mom to take him back. I thought Mom was going to let him in, but she didn't. She called the cops right away 'cause he's not supposed to get near our apartment. They came and took Dad away."

"I'm glad your Mom was strong enough to make that decision."

"Yeah, me too," Rina said, raising her voice slightly. "And I hope Dad never comes back again."

The anger in Rina's voice bothered me, but I knew it would take time for it to disappear. "Now, when are you coming to see me again?"

"That's what I was calling you about."

It pleased me to know that Rina was the one who was initiating the next meeting between us. I had certainly missed talking with her, but it was important that Rina recognized the value of our counseling sessions.

"How does next Thursday after school sound?"

"Sure, Ms. Martínez," Rina happily agreed. "And I have a new poem I wrote that I'd like to show you."

"That's great—I can hardly wait to read it. But meanwhile, if you or your mom need anything, feel free to call me at home."

"Thanks, Ms. Martínez," Rina said.

As I hung up the receiver, I paused, smiling to myself. I was delighted with Rina's willingness to share her poetry with me. And although I knew it was going to be a long, bumpy road ahead, there was no doubt in my mind that Rina and her mom were going to piece their life back together again.

GLOSSARY

¿A dónde vas, hija?—Where are you going, my daughter?

Andale, hija—Go ahead, daughter.

Ay, m'ija—Oh, my daughter.

baboso—Idiot; dummy; "saliva-face."

barrio—Latino neighborhood.

Bien truchas—Pretty bad; awesome.

Bueno, hija—Well, my daughter.

caldo—Mexican soup made of beef and vegetables.

Cállate—Be quiet.

chica loca—Crazy girl.

Chicanos—Persons of Mexican descent raised in the United States.

chile verde—Green chile.

cholo/chola—Contemporary Chicano youth who dress distinctively and rebel against mainstream culture.

cochino—Pig, slob.

comadre—Protector (female); close family friend; a relative "by mutual consent," who may or may not be of blood relation.

compadre—Protector (male); close family friend; a relative "by mutual consent" who may or may not be of blood relation.

¡Cómo no! Andale, vieja—But of course! Come on, old lady.

¿Cómo te fue en la escuela, hija?—How was school today, my daughter?

¿Dónde andabas?—Where were you?

El Vez—Popular Chicano singer known as "the Mexican Elvis."
Es la culpa de tu mamá—It's your mother's fault.
esa—Greeting which means "homegirl" (slang).
ese—Greeting which means "homeboy" (slang).
¡Estás bien loco (loca)!—You're really crazy.
!Estupendo!—Wonderful! Great!

gabacho—Anglo-American.

hijo—Son.

Lalo Guerrero—Emmy award-winning songwriter and musician who was born in Tucson, Arizona and is considered the Godfather of Chicano music; recipient of the National Medal of the Arts Award.
los niños—The children.

maleducada—Rude, ill-mannered.
mami—Mommy.
mentiroso, mentirosa—Liar.
mexicano, mexicana—Someone of Mexican descent.
m'ijo, m'ija—the contraction of "my son" or "my daughter."
mocoso, mocosa—Snot-nosed boy or girl; sometimes used endearingly.

Orale—Hey; okay; right on; all right.

panza—Belly.
panzón (es)—Fatso; a big-bellied person.
papi—Daddy.

pachuco talk—The dialect Caló or the speech style of *pachucos* and *cholos*—that is, a mixture of Spanish and English.

pendejo, pendeja—idiot; fool; a stupid person.

Póngase trucha—Be smart; get with it.

Qué bueno, hija—That's good, my daughter.

¿Qué te pasa, hija?—What's wrong, my daughter?

ruca—chick; babe; homegirl.

¡Suéltame, José! Por el amor de Dios, suéltame!—Let me go, José! For the love of God, let me go!

telenovela—Soap operas.

Tío—Uncle.

Titi—Aunt.

¡Ven acá!—Come here!

verduras—Vegetables.

viejitos—Little old people.

Zora Neale Hurston—African-American novelist, folklorist and anthropologist from the "Harlem Renaissance" period of the 1920s.